DEVOURED

AVA THORNE

For those who know that monsters often wear human faces.

And to all the women who came before me. Thank you for fighting so that I could write smut about a spider demon.

Content Warning

This book contains the following content that some users may find disturbing. Please read at your own discretion.

- Explicit sexual content
- Suicidal ideation
- Gore
- PTSD
- Body horror/transformation
- SA of a main character (not explicitly described, not by MMC)
- Memory of SA
- Torture of main character
- Harm by a trusted individual
- Bondage and suspension
- Double penetration
- Knotting
- Monster fucking
- Toxic relationship dynamics/obsession

- Death of animals (hunting)
- Cannibalism (monsters eating humans)

Chapter 1

Flavia

Outside Bath, England 143 CE

The lake stretched before me like a dark mirror, its surface so still it might have been polished obsidian. The moon hung—full and yellow—over the black waters. Its sickly light turned my hair to silver threads that caught and held the darkness between them as I sat on the stone steps of the villa's eastern terrace. My bare feet dangled just above the dry grass of late autumn, and I wondered if tonight would be the night I finally found the courage to use the knife hidden beneath my stola.

The blade was a small kitchen thing I'd stolen three nights earlier, after my husband, Tiberius, had left me crumpled on the foyer floor, blood seeping into the expensive mosaic depicting Medusa's severed head. *How fitting*, I had thought through the haze of pain. The monster's azure eyes had stared up at me from the floor while monsters wearing human faces looked down.

I'd dreamed I was her once, when I still fought back. I imagined serpents wrapping around my husband's neck as I squeezed the life from him. But unlike the Gorgon, I could not turn my tormentors to stone. She had been punished for being violated, transformed into something terrible for crimes committed against her. I could only bleed and endure and dream of an ending to the pain—any ending. Now, all my dreams were nothing but nightmares.

Behind me, the villa sprawled in all its imperial splendor: forty-three rooms of heated floors and painted walls, baths that steamed with water brought through ingenious Roman engineering, and corridors lined with stolen treasures from lands that no longer existed.

I was one of those treasures.

It should have been a palace. Instead, it was my tomb—a beautiful, expensive tomb where I rotted alive, breath by breath, day by day.

The hypocaust system that heated the tiles hummed beneath the floors like some great beast's breathing. The furnace pumped hot air through the villa to drive away the chill of the northern climate. I knew those heated chambers too well. Tiberius—my dear husband—enjoyed the way a hot tile could sear skin, the way screams echoed differently in the underground room that held the furnace. The villa's luxury was a lie; every comfort had been perverted into an instrument of torment. Even now, I could smell the lingering scent of burning flesh that no amount of frankincense could mask.

I shifted on the cold stone, welcoming the bite of chill against my skin. Cold was honest. Cold was clean. Cold numbed the constellation of injuries that mapped my body like some twisted cartographer's chart of suffering.

The burn on my left shoulder blade still wept beneath the thin fabric of my stola—a gift from Tiberius' heated brooch. My ribs ached where Marcus, Tiberius' second in command, had kicked me yesterday for spilling wine. Worse were the thin cuts that laced my arms and legs like some perverse form of decoration. Gaius, barely old enough to need a razor, took pleasure in his blade's work. He carved shallow lines with a artist's hand—never deep enough to truly damage, only to hurt. Only to remind me that my body belonged to them, to mark however they chose.

But it was the ache between my legs that shamed me most, that hollow, burning throb that spoke of the night's earlier entertainment. Three of them this time, taking turns while Tiberius watched and offered commentary like some depraved instructor. The pain radiated through my pelvis with each shift of position, a deep wrongness that made my stomach clench with nausea. I should have been used to it by now—the gods knew it happened often enough—but the shame never lessened. The first time, I'd bitten off one of the men's fingers. It had only made it worse, and the lashing I received afterward nearly killed me. I'd learned it was better to sink into my mind, a place they could not touch. When it was just me and my songs, no one could hurt me.

My mother would weep to see what had become of her daughter. Though perhaps she would understand. She had been a slave before my father married her. Had she not suffered similarly before death claimed her? Had she not whispered warnings about wolves in men's clothing, about the price of beauty in a world that devours the vulnerable?

The old gods still walk, hidden in the shadows, my mother's voice whispered in memory. *When the wind carries the scent of eternity, it means the veil grows thin.* It had been a warning to stay inside on the night of Samhain. To light fires to keep away the demons that lurked.

But fire brought me no comfort now. So as the moon hung

full on the evening when the veil grew thin, I prayed to fall through that veil and never be seen again.

My mother was seven years dead, claimed by fever. Her death had perhaps been a relief to my father. He had shamed himself by marrying a Briton slave who spoke too often of the old ways, who traced protective symbols in the air when she thought no one was watching, and whose wildness was never truly hidden.

Now only I remained, and my Roman name, Flavia, sat bitter on my tongue. Flavia—the golden one, named by my father for the hair that had doomed both my mother and me. Hair that caught light like spun gold in daylight and silver in moonbeams. Something rare, and therefore coveted. Hair that had made my mother beautiful enough to claim, and me cursed enough to keep. *Moon-blessed*, she had whispered once, running gentle fingers through my pale strands. *Moon-cursed*, I corrected, for what blessing had it ever brought but pain?

The wind picked up again, stronger than before, and with it came a sound like whispers—or perhaps breathing. Massive oaks beyond the lake's far shore swayed, their ancient branches creaking like old bones. The forest stretched dark and deep beyond them, older than Rome itself, older than human memory. The wildwood, which even Rome could not tame. Even the legions avoided its heart, claiming savage beasts and the ghosts of conquered tribes haunted it.

The truth was far worse. The slaves called him the Devourer—a man-eater—when they dared speak of him at all. A demon who wore human shape until the moment he shed it. No one who entered the forest's depths ever returned, though sometimes hunters found tracks that began as a man's footprints and ended as something else entirely—something with too many joints, too many limbs.

The Devourer suffered from endless hunger, and he would consume us all without sacrifice—or so the stories said. *To appease him, the old tribes gave him brides. Only the most beautiful girls would he take. They became his, body and soul, and in return...* My mother's words flowed like dark honey in my memory. *And in exchange for that bargain, their homes were spared.*

It had not been a comforting bedtime story, but I saw now that perhaps it wasn't meant to be. It was a warning—of the appetites of men and the price for denying them.

I looked out into the dark woods again. Was it just a story to keep children tucked in bed at night? Looking into those deep shadows, I doubted it. If monsters dwelled in homes and villas, why wouldn't they live in the heart of woods more ancient than man himself?

How hungry was he now? Years without sacrifice, with the old tribes scattered from these lands, and only the scraps that dared wander through the woods to eat. Was he starved—desperate, driven mad by his hunger?

My hand closed around the knife's handle beneath the wool of my stola. The metal was cold against my palm, but not as cold as the certainty crystallizing in my chest like winter ice. Had I been driven mad, craving the escape of death from my endless pain? Was I any different from that demon in the woods?

The wind whipped my hair, and the fresh cuts on my arms stung as my lower belly throbbed. Yes—they had driven me to madness. I would not be their plaything any longer.

The wind gusted again, and this time I was certain I heard something calling from across the dark water. Not words, precisely, but something that made my blood sing with recognition.

Come to me, the wind whispered, carrying with it the scent of dark earth and old magic. *Come to me, moon-blessed daughter. Come to me, and learn what hunger truly feels like.*

I rose slowly, my legs unsteady from the day's fresh bruises. The stone step felt like ice beneath my bare feet, but I welcomed it. The forest seemed closer now, though I knew that was impossible. My ancestors' songs rang in my ears—of dark waters that served as doorways, of lakes that had no bottom because they opened onto the Otherworld.

Beware the waters, beware their calling sound.
Turn back, my love, or you'll be drowned.

The knife's weight in my hand felt suddenly insignificant. What was one small blade against the enormity of my suffering? What was one quick cut against years of slow dying? The dark lake called me to the Otherworld—to a place where suffering ended, where I could be wrapped in cold until I was numb to everything.

I took a step toward the lake's edge, then another. The water lapped gently at the shore, dark as spilled blood in the moonlight. My toes breached the surface, and the cold was so deep it burned. But it was a burn that would end.

"Stop, Flavia."

A voice cut through the night air, and my blood turned to ice in my veins. I knew that voice. Knew the particular mixture of amusement and ownership that colored each syllable of my hated name.

Tiberius.

I didn't turn around. If I did, I'd lose what little courage I had. Instead, I took another step into the water, toward the calling of the wind, toward the darkness.

"I said, stop." His voice was closer now, boots clicking against the stone tiles. "Step away from the water. Now."

Come, before it's too late. Before they drag you back to die slowly in their heated halls.

But firm hands seized my shoulders before I could take another step, fingers digging into tender bruises. Tiberius spun me around to face him, his dark eyes glittering with anticipation that made my stomach clench with familiar dread.

"Did you think I wouldn't notice you'd left your room?" he murmured, his breath wine-sweet against my face. "Did you think I wouldn't find you here, contemplating something foolish?"

His gaze dropped to the knife in my hand, and his smile widened. With casual ease, he twisted my wrist until my fingers spasmed open and the blade clattered to the tiles at our feet. The sound echoed across the water like a death knell.

"Tsk, tsk," he said, genuine amusement in his voice. "Were you planning to use that on yourself? Or perhaps..." His smile turned savage. "Were you planning to use it on me?"

I didn't answer. The calling in the wind was fading now, growing distant as he dragged me backward—away from the lake, away from the forest, away from the only hope I'd known in months.

"Come," Tiberius said, his grip tightening until I could feel bones grinding together. "My men are waiting, and the night is still young. We have such wonderful games planned for you."

Fear squeezed my heart until I thought it might burst. Dread crept through me, my familiar companion. I would not let it show. I had learned long ago that only made what came next far worse.

As he hauled me back toward the villa's heat, I cast one last desperate look toward the dark forest beyond the lake. The trees swayed in a wind I could no longer feel, and for just a moment, I swore I saw something move between their trunks.

The hypocaust system breathed as Tiberius led me deeper into the torch-lit corridors, back to the rooms where pain had its own language and mercy was a word long forgotten. Heat surrounded me until clammy sweat covered my whole body. The air was still and smothering, and—despite my best efforts —my body shook, knowing what came next.

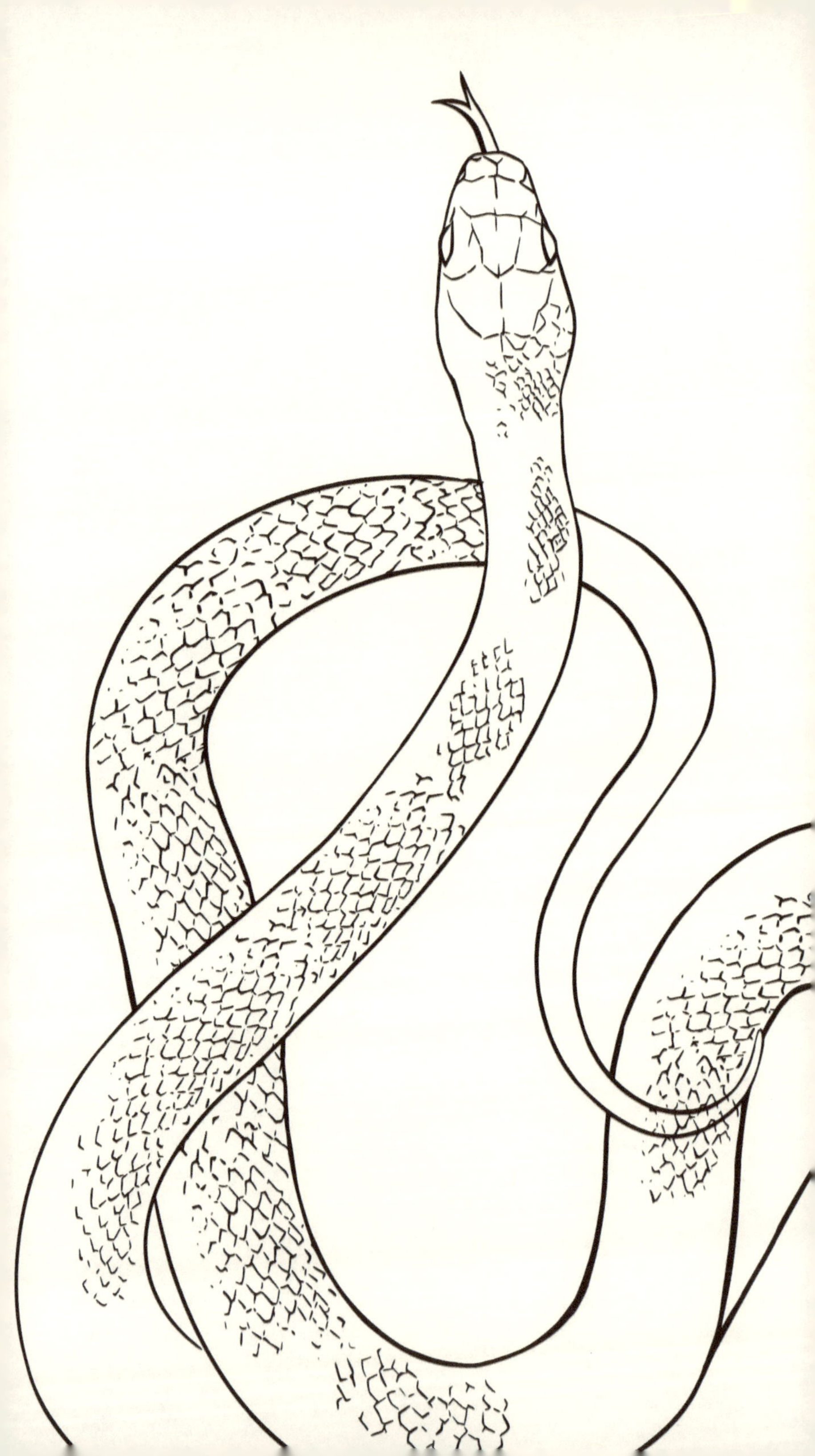

CHAPTER 2

—————

FLAVIA

The villa's triclinium flickered with torchlight and shadows, the flames casting mocking figures on the frescoed walls. Tiberius' cohort sprawled across the couches like feeding wolves, wine already darkening their lips and loosening their tongues. I could smell the familiar scent of heated metal from the braziers where Tiberius kept his...tools.

They had arranged themselves on the low couches like vultures settling to feast. Tiberius reclined in the place of honor, his toga pristine despite the late hour, dark eyes tracking my movement with the focused attention of a snake watching a mouse. Marcus lounged to his left, thick fingers already working at his belt, while young Gaius perched on the edge of his couch like an eager hound scenting prey.

Three others I didn't recognize filled the remaining spaces —new faces drawn by Tiberius' promise of exotic entertainment. Fresh appetites to feed. Fresh eyes to witness my degradation.

"Our little Briton looks pale tonight," Marcus observed, his words slurring slightly. "Perhaps she needs warming."

"Then let us not keep her waiting." Tiberius snapped his fingers. "Strip her."

Hands tore at my stola before I could move, rough fingers catching on fresh scabs and old scars alike. The fabric gave way violently, and then I stood naked before them, my pale skin mapped with the geography of their previous attentions. I could feel their eyes crawling over every exposed inch of flesh like hungry beasts.

Someone whistled low. "You've been thorough, Tiberius."

"One must be, with the wild ones." Tiberius rose from his couch, circling me slowly. "They require...careful handling. Don't you, my dear Flavia?"

I said nothing. Long experience had taught me that words only gave them more ammunition, more excuses for creative punishments. But my silence seemed to amuse him more than any protest would have tonight.

"How Caelus ever thought I would sully my bloodline with a barbarian like you is beyond me. That he did shows he was never worthy of his title. A disgrace to Rome. Still, the bride price was too good to pass up."

If he thought insulting my father would rile me, he was mistaken. He should have known that by now, yet a frown tugged at his lips.

"There's something different about you tonight," he mused, reaching out to run a finger along my jaw. "Something..."

The wind outside suddenly gusted hard enough to rattle the shutters, and all the oil lamps flickered. In the dancing shadows, I could have sworn I saw a face looking back. Then I smelled it again—that wild, ancient scent from the lake. Earth and moss and beneath that, something wicked and hungry.

Tiberius' hand tightened on my chin. "No matter. We have games to play."

"It's Samhain," whispered Gaius, and the sound made the cuts on my arms tingle. "The Briton barbarians believe the dead walk tonight."

"Foolish beasts. Bring her here," Tiberius commanded, and hands—too many hands—reached for me. Marcus' fingers found the tender spot beneath my ribs, pressing until I gasped. Gaius traced one of his careful slices with a fingertip, smiling at my flinch.

I let my mind drift then, as I had learned to do—let it float away from the heated tools and grasping hands, away from the laughter that followed each small sound of pain I couldn't suppress. Instead, I thought of the lake in moonlight, of the dark forest beyond where everything was cold and silent.

Songs rose to cut through the pain, but one was louder than the rest tonight:

> *When moonlight calls across the mere,*
> *beware the Devourer drawing near.*
>
> *Within the wildwood he waits alone,*
> *to swallow you whole, blood and bone.*
>
> *Strike your bargain with curse and plea,*
> *he'll take your price, but none go free.*
>
> *So guard your sorrow, maiden fair,*
> *lest eight-legged shadows taste despair.*

"The Devourer feeds on despair," my mother's voice whispered in memory. "When the veil thins, he grows stronger."

But what was the Devourer compared to this? What was one ancient hunger against the daily feast these monsters made of my suffering?

The men spoke around me and through me as if I weren't there, discussing their plans with the casual cruelty of those who had forgotten what it meant to see suffering and feel shame.

"—stretch it out this time—"

"—the heated rod worked well last—"

"—see how long before she breaks—"

The wind rose again, and this time I heard something else in it—a calling, deep and thrumming. A new song that sounded like destruction.

"She's not listening," one of them complained. "Look at her eyes. She's gone somewhere else."

A hand struck my cheek, sharp enough to bring tears, and I was dragged back to the heated floor and circle of leering faces.

"Better," Tiberius said, his fingers tangling in my moon-cursed hair. "We want you present for this, wife. We want you to remember every moment."

They always did. They fed on the memory as much as the moment, taking pleasure in how I would flinch days later at a sudden sound, how my hands would shake when I heard their footsteps in the corridors.

But something was different this time. As Marcus pressed my face into the mosaic tiles, as Gaius' knife traced patterns in my flesh, as hands and mouths and worse violated every boundary—something inside me began to shift.

The pain was there, sharp and immediate as always. But beneath it, something else stirred. A hunger that wasn't mine. A rage that tasted of ancient forests and forgotten gods. When Gaius cut too deep and blood ran hot down my leg, I found myself thinking not of escape but of teeth—of how fragile his throat looked, of how easily it would tear.

The thought should have horrified me. Instead, it sang through my veins like ice.

"She's not crying," one of the strangers observed, sounding vaguely disappointed. "Usually they cry by now."

Tiberius studied me with those cold eyes. I lay crumpled on the blood-smeared tiles, every inch of me a symphony of pain, but he was right—no tears came. Only that strange hunger, growing stronger with each heartbeat.

"Perhaps we've finally broken her completely," Marcus suggested, giving me a final kick that sent white-hot agony through my ribs.

"No," Tiberius said slowly. "No, I don't think so."

He crouched beside me, gripping my hair to force my head up. This close, I could see the fine lines around his eyes, could smell the wine on his breath mixed with something else—was that fear? Just a trace, but unmistakable.

"What are you thinking, wife?" he whispered. "What goes on behind those witch-eyes?"

I smiled then, blood dripping from my mouth. I couldn't help it. Because at that moment, with pain singing through every nerve, I knew without a doubt what I would do. I was tired of being prey. Tired of flinching at footsteps, of anticipating pain, of praying to gods who either didn't exist or simply didn't care. Roman gods, pagan gods—what difference did it make? None had answered my prayers for mercy or death or even simple sleep free from nightmares.

But perhaps there was another kind of prayer. Perhaps what I needed wasn't a god at all, but a demon.

I heard it clearly—the calling from the forest. *Come to me,* it whispered. *Come and learn what it means to be the one who devours.*

I closed my eyes and let the call wash through me like dark water, drowning the sound of laughter and bite of pain.

Devour them, I thought as the shadows deepened. *Devour me.*

For the first time in months—perhaps years—I fought back. I dragged my nails down Tiberius' face and watched as small bubbles of red appeared in their path. He staggered away, his expression twisting.

"Barbarian bitch. She's all yours now, men."

Hands gripped harder, wrenching apart my legs as the night's true entertainment began. But even as I let my mind flee the heated chamber and its human monsters, I held tight to that silver thread of hunger.

I wasn't strong enough to fight them all, to even truly hurt them. But there was someone who could, someone who would devour them all.

And in the wind's answering howl, I heard laughter—but not human laughter. Something unhinged and slow, that spoke of hungers older than Rome and vengeance sharper than any blade these mortal monsters could imagine.

Darkness enveloped me, cold and comforting, as I swore to myself that no matter the cost, I would have my revenge. Even if that cost was my life.

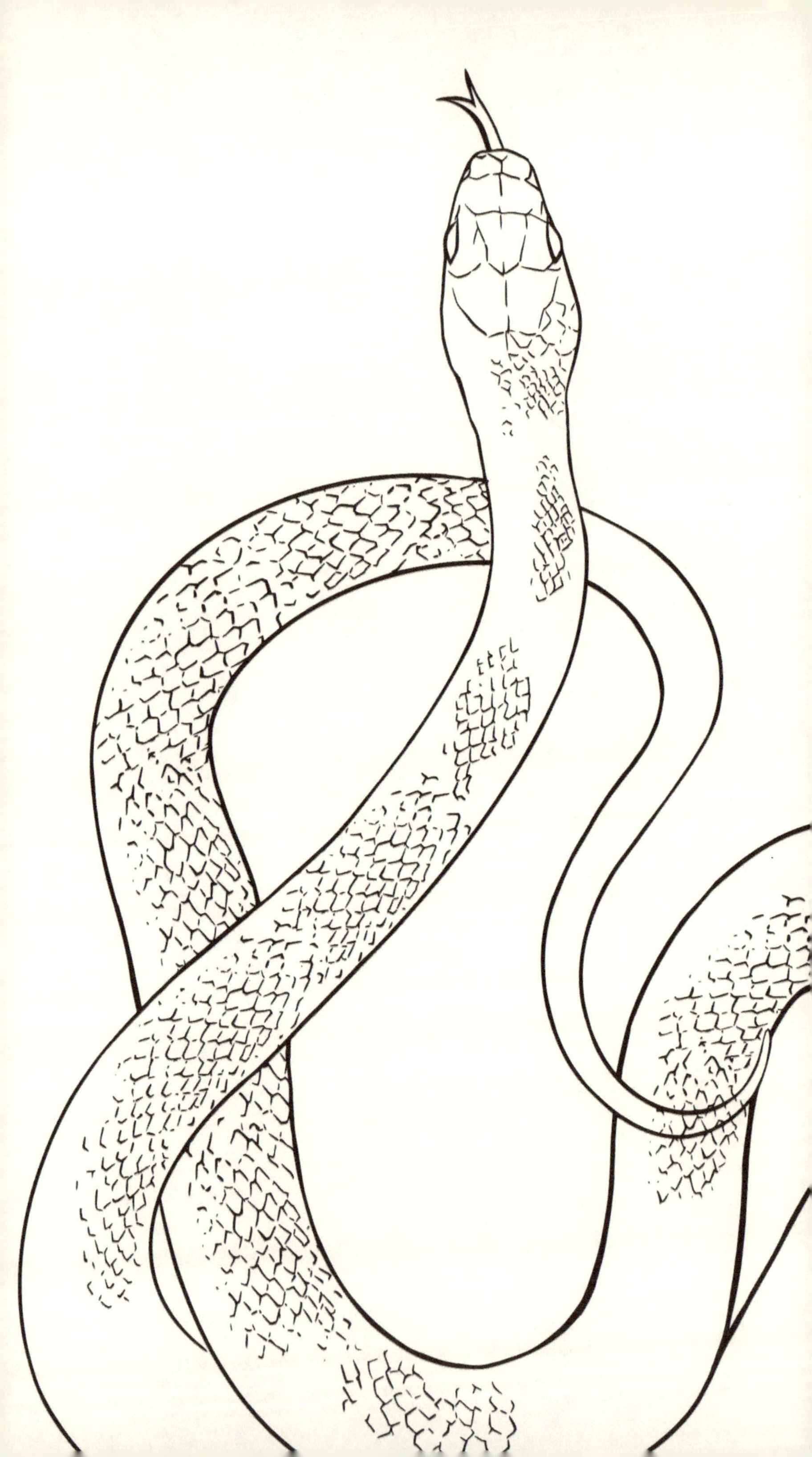

CHAPTER 3

FLAVIA

I woke in the early hours of the morning, my face stuck to the tiled floor with wine and dried blood. They had been drinking heavily and had grown bored quickly tonight, leaving me in my state of dissociation long before the moon had set.

Marcus and the others had worn themselves out early, but Gaius had lingered. The new cuts on my arms stung, but after I'd stopped responding, he'd pulled one of the new slave girls into his room. I could still hear her faint crying in the distance.

I pushed myself up on straining limbs and hobbled to the nearest window, flinging open the shutters.

The terrible heat of the room was cut by the frigid night air, and I gazed up at the full moon now hanging just over the treetops. It was red. A blood moon on Samhain was a sign that the spirits hungered.

The cold air bit into my wounds, but I welcomed it. Pain meant I was still alive, still capable of choice. The blood moon hung heavy above the forest, painting everything in shades of rust and shadow. *When the harvest moon bleeds, the old paths reveal themselves to those who dare to walk them.*

I gathered nothing but the clothes on my back. There would be no return from this journey. But I would escape. My death would be my own. My bare feet swept along the floor without a sound; years of trying to avoid notice had taught me how to move like smoke through these halls.

The villa's eastern gate was guarded, but the guards were deep in their cups, celebrating Samhain in the Roman fashion —with wine and dice rather than the proper reverence the night demanded. I slipped past them like a ghost, my pale hair covered with a stolen cloak.

The lake stretched before me, its surface turned to molten copper under the blood moon's gaze. I didn't pause at its shore this time. The calling came from deeper, from the ancient heart of the forest where Roman roads feared to venture. I skirted the water's edge, following game trails and clinging to the shadows.

The tree line loomed overhead, but as I drew closer, some-thing changed. There—between two massive oaks—a gap that shouldn't exist. The darkness there was different, older, breathing with its own rhythm. And at its threshold, I saw them: the marker stones.

Three standing stones, each no higher than my knee, worn smooth by centuries of wind and rain. But the symbols carved into them were still clear in the blood moon's light—spirals and serpents and eight-legged shapes that seemed to dance across the stone.

The old paths remember those who remember them, Mother had whispered. *Blood calls to blood, hunger to hunger.*

Between the stones, the forest floor was different. Where everywhere else lay thick with fallen leaves and undergrowth, here was a path of packed earth, worn smooth by pilgrims on a doomed quest. How long had it been since someone had last walked this path, heading straight toward their demise?

I knelt at the threshold, my wounds singing in pain, and placed one trembling hand on the center stone. The carved spider seemed to pulse beneath my palm, and for a moment I could have sworn I felt it move, eight legs shifting in welcome —or warning.

The wind rose, and the trees groaned and swayed, their branches creating a tunnel of shadow over the hidden path.

Behind me, I heard the distant sounds of the villa—a shout of laughter, the crash of something breaking, a servant girl's muffled sobs carried on the night air. Ahead lay only darkness and the promise of something worse than death.

Or perhaps something better than the slow dying I'd endured for so long.

I rose on unsteady legs, pulled the cloak tighter around my shoulders, and stepped between the stones onto the ancient path. The moment my feet touched that strangely warm earth, the sounds of the Roman world faded as if swallowed by thick wool. There was only the forest now, only the blood moon's light filtering through branches that seemed to reach for me with grasping fingers.

The path wound into the darkness like a snake losing itself in the long grass. Each turn was obscured by the trees before it, and the part of my mind that was always looking for danger was screaming. My body knew I wasn't Flavia at all. I was prey.

The woods were loud, the leaf litter rustling with the sound of thousands of small feet. Creatures of all kinds watched me from the darkness, and I felt the pressure of count-less tiny glowing eyes.

What a fool you are, they seemed to say. *Turn back while you still can.*

The moonlight solidified into silver threads, guiding me forward. Guiding me to my doom—and my salvation.

They wound deeper still, past trees whose trunks were wider than the villa's walls, their bark etched with symbols I didn't understand. I didn't need to know their meaning to comprehend their power—spirals and knots that spoke of old magic, wilder than these woods.

Between the trees, small lights danced. Will-o'-the-wisps, calling me deeper. They were old magic spirits, and I found comfort in them. Had they come out to see me to my journey's end? My heart slowed, and the panic that had been rising in my chest subsided. The magic of my mother's people was all around me. A small comfort, but a comfort nonetheless.

I followed the glowing trail, and white flowers began to litter the forest floor. In the pale moonlight, I couldn't identify them. They glittered in the silver light, delicate petals scattered like offerings. I stepped carefully among them, unwilling to disturb their fragile beauty.

The lights danced closer, weaving between the trees. I reached out to one, enchanted by its golden glow, and my fingers brushed against something I couldn't see. Something thin and sticky pulled at my hand.

I jerked back, but more strands caught my arm, my shoulder. The dancing lights weren't wisps at all—they were fireflies, dozens of them, trapped in threads so fine they were nearly invisible. Their struggles made them flicker and dance, creating the illusion of guiding spirits.

The white "flowers" beneath my feet crunched wrong. Too hard for petals. I looked down, and my stomach turned—not flowers but bones, small ones, scattered and bleached by time.

Bird bones, rodent bones—creatures who had once been caught in this trap.

Just as I had.

I tried to retreat, but more threads ensnared me—in my hair, across my waist, tangling my legs. The silver moonlight hadn't been a beautiful shadow at all. It had been illuminating a web so vast it filled the spaces between trees, so perfectly woven it appeared a mere trick of light until you were already caught.

I thrashed, tearing through the silk. The threads were stronger than they looked, but they gave way under my frantic pulling. Fireflies tumbled free around me, their light fading as they fled. More web caught me even as I destroyed it, and I realized with growing horror that I was moving deeper, not escaping.

The ground suddenly wasn't there.

I plunged through the curtain of web into open space, landing hard on ground carpeted thick with bones--not small ones now, but human-sized, some still wrapped in tattered cloth. The impact drove the air from my lungs, and I lay gasping among the dead, looking up at a dome of silver silk that blocked out the stars.

The web above was a masterwork—art and trap all at once. Threads as thick as rope formed the main structure, while finer strands wove between them in purposeful geometric patterns. And caught in this deadly masterpiece hung cocoons of wrapped silk—some small, some the size of boar, and some...some very distinctly human-shaped. Dozens of these victims hung over my head, the web still singing with vibrations from my fall, and from somewhere in the shadows came a sound like laughter—or just the wind through old, hollow bones.

I had found my destination, though not as I'd intended. The Devourer's grove had caught its newest prey.

I stood in the center of that terrible beauty, surrounded by the remains of whoever had come before me, and felt the weight of ancient eyes upon my skin. I understood now that I had been guided here as surely as any fly drawn to its doom.

But I was no unwilling victim. I had come seeking this place, seeking him. And as the shadows between the trees began to coalesce into something that might have been a figure, I lifted my chin and spoke the name my mother had whispered in the old tongue.

"Ysu."

The web above shivered in response, and from the darkness came that same sound again—but now it was clearly a deep, amused chuckle.

It was accompanied by the scurry of a thousand jointed legs, and the forest floor around me moved in waves as spiders scurried away from the darkness looming before me.

"What prey has wandered into my web tonight?"

A deep voice echoed from the space between the trees, so resonant I felt it in my bones.

"I come to make a bargain with you, Devourer."

The darkness between the ancient oaks shifted, and he emerged from that primordial shadow.

The spiders that had carpeted the bone-strewn ground parted before him like subjects before a sovereign. Some were as large as dinner plates, others no bigger than coins, but all fled with the same urgent reverence.

When he finally stepped into the grove's spectral light, I understood why my mother's stories had always ended in warnings.

The Devourer stood taller than any man should, his frame

broad in ways that suggested not mere muscle but something denser, more substantial than mortal flesh. His skin held the grayish pallor of deep cave mushrooms—of things that grew in places where sunlight was merely rumor. But it was the marks that drew my eye: black patterns that crawled across his exposed flesh like living things, organic whorls and spirals that seemed to shift when I wasn't looking directly at them. They weren't tattoos or scars but something integral to his being, as if darkness itself had taken root beneath his skin and bloomed into these terrible designs.

His face might have been handsome once, in the way ancient gods possessed a cruel beauty. Sharp cheekbones cast shadows too deep for the available light, and his jaw held a severe, angular severity. But his mouth—his mouth was too wide, the corners extending just slightly beyond where human anatomy should have allowed, giving every expression a manic cast that made my stomach clench in trepidation.

A dark robe draped over his shoulders, hanging with an unnatural stillness despite the night breeze stirring the leaves above, and something about its fall suggested it concealed more than it revealed. The way it bunched at odd angles, the subtle movement beneath its folds that didn't match his visible motions—my mind shied away from what else it might hide.

He settled on an ancient stump that nature had carved into something resembling a throne, the wood so old it had taken on the quality of stone. The ease with which he claimed it, the way his presence seemed to transform dead wood into a seat of power, spoke of centuries of dominion. His thick legs crossed with casual elegance, but even in repose he radiated the coiled potential of a predator merely choosing not to strike.

Yet it was his eyes that truly betrayed his nature. In the glow of his web, they appeared almost entirely black, but as he tilted his head to study me, I caught glimpses of something worse—pupils that reflected light like a cat's, with the same vertical slit. When he blinked, it wasn't quite synchronized, as though multiple sets of eyes shared the same sockets, taking turns to observe the world behind that almost-human face.

"A bargain." His voice, when he spoke again, carried harmonics that resonated in my chest cavity. "How refreshingly direct. Most who find their way here merely scream or beg. Tell me, little human, what it is you desire from me?"

He looked down at me, resting his chin on one hand, his face cracking into that too-wide grin.

"Revenge."

Those unnatural eyes surveyed me. "Revenge? How very human. And who has wronged you so deeply that you would seek me out?"

My fists balled at my sides. "My husband and his men."

"Ah, yes. I thought I smelled those Roman fools on you. So the pretty little human is married to a brute." He held so unnaturally still—a spider waiting for me to fall into his trap. "And you desire my aid in what? Killing them all?"

"Yes." I didn't break eye contact with him, despite how very wrong those black eyes were.

"You come here seeking a boon but carry no purse or treasures. I wonder...what is it you intend to trade with me?"

The grin that split his face told me he knew what I intended, but wanted me to debase myself by saying it. Fine. I would play his game. Any shame I had was burned away by my husband long ago.

"I trade myself. I offer myself as your bride."

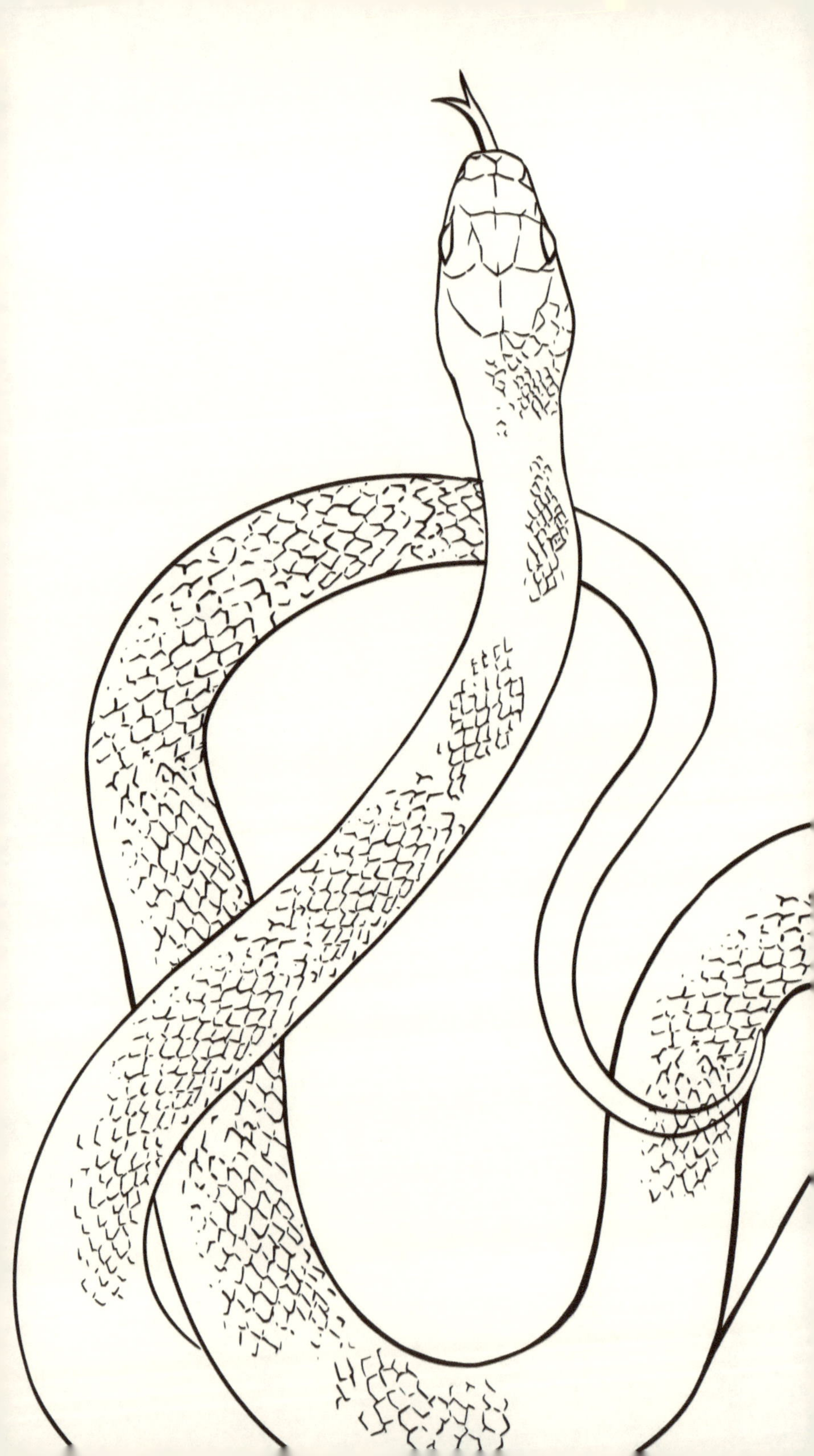

CHAPTER 4

FLAVIA

There was a long pause, and then he laughed. It was a slow, mocking sound that rumbled deep in my belly as heat and something much darker mixed.

"You think yourself my equal? To be my bride? Quite bold for a human. Perhaps I will let you tell me more of these jokes before I eat you."

Before I could react, he was on me, his too-large hand wrapped completely around my face like a vise. My hands clung to his forearm, iron-hard beneath my fingers, as he lifted me into the air. My feet swung freely as I struggled, and I watched in horror as a dark tongue far too long to be human lashed from his mouth, tasting the air between us.

"Let us be honest with each other, little human. I do so hate how humans refuse to say what they truly mean. You say you will be my bride, but what you *mean* is that you will give me your body to debase however I see fit." His hand tightened until I could barely breathe.

"And there are so many ways in which I could ruin you. Your body is so small, so fragile. How easily I could break you while I pumped you full of my venom and my cum, until you were bursting and begging me for more."

I shivered as his words caressed my ear, a grotesque imitation of a lover's whisper. It was fear—I was no fool. But what he didn't know was there was no pain he could inflict that I had not already suffered, no horror worse than what waited for me back in that villa. I feared him, but I had killed the part of myself that reacted to fear a long time ago.

"Yes," I rasped. "That is what I offer you."

Something hot and wet snaked up the side of my neck, that horrible squelching sound echoing in my ear as I forced myself not to squirm, not to give him the satisfaction.

Then it halted abruptly, and he dropped me. My knees buckled as I hit the ground, splitting open on the forest floor. He turned his back on me, waving one hand dismissively.

"Unfortunately for you, bodies—especially human bodies —are cheap. Expendable. You would trade me one for the near hundred you wish me to slaughter? No. That is no trade at all."

I was so stunned I barely felt the pain in my knees. I hadn't expected him to ask for more. Mother had warned never to let a demon suggest a price—it would always be too high. But I was past the point where the cost mattered. My death was imminent; I was merely negotiating the method.

"What do you want, then?"

He was on me again in a flash, his hand crushing my throat as he pressed me into the ground with the weight of his body. His face was so close I could see the slight difference between the darkness of his irises and the black of his pupils.

"Bodies are cheap, but the mind...now that is a valuable thing. And yet I think even that is not enough in this case."

He grinned, that too-wide grin, and his elongated fangs flashed in the moonlight.

"No. For what you ask, I would need your soul, little human."

"My soul? How can I—"

"You will be mine—mind, body, and soul. You will obey me, my every whim. Should I desire you kneel, you kneel. Should I desire your mouth on my cocks, your tongue will ache for the taste. Should I wish to hang you from the trees and slowly consume the delicious nectar of your liquified insides, you will accept it. *That* is how you give me your soul. Obedience without question to any and all of my desires."

So he was no different than any other man. Control. But at least he was honest. I would move from a heated cage to an ancient one—but I would have my revenge. I could never kill the men in my villa alone. But he could. And once he had, I would escape, even if that escape was death.

"I agree," I said without hesitation.

He pulled back slightly.

"You are either very brave, very stupid, or pathetically desperate."

"You've named your price, and I accept. What else could you want?"

"Look at me, little human. Really *look* at me."

I held his gaze, and as I did, another set of eyes opened beneath the dark ones that already pinned me. Then another. And another. Despite my best efforts, I gasped.

The new eyes were smaller than the human pair, clustered like black gems along what I had thought was merely shadow under his cheekbones. They blinked in a ripple of obsidian, reflecting the web's ethereal glow. Each pupil caught the light differently, creating the unsettling impression that he was seeing me from multiple angles at once, studying me with the calculating patience of a predator who had all the time in the world.

He chuckled. "Oh, you haven't seen anything yet."

His robe flew back with a whisper of fabric, and I saw four more arms unfurl from his sides like some terrible flowering. They weren't human—black and segmented, covered in a chitinous shell that gleamed with oily iridescence. The joints made a soft clicking sound as they moved, each segment grinding against the next with a noise that echoed with death. The ends tapered to points sharp enough to pierce armor, serrated edges glinting as they flexed.

The additional limbs moved with their own intelligence, independent of his human arms. One reached toward me, tracing down my cheek with a surprisingly gentle touch.

"Scared?" The word carried amusement, but underneath it pulsed something hungrier.

"No." The lie came easier than breath. I had learned long ago that showing fear only fed the appetites of monsters, whether they wore human faces or revealed their true nature beneath the moon.

He shook his head, and the motion sent ripples through his additional eyes. "All humans do is lie."

He pulled back, and for a moment I thought perhaps he had accepted my bravado. But then that deep chittering returned—louder now, insistent. It seemed to come from everywhere at once: the web above, the bones below, the very air between us. The sound burrowed into my bones, a vibration speaking of hunger as ancient as the forest itself.

The shadows around him began to shift and dance, not cast by any earthly light but flowing from his very being. His form stretched upward, growing taller—but wrong, all wrong.

His human legs dissolved into darkness, replaced by something birthing itself from shadow.

A massive black carapace unfolded beneath him, broad as a table and segmented like armor forged in the depths of some infernal smithy. From it emerged eight legs—true spider legs—each longer than I was tall. They moved in a staccato of motion, each step whisper-quiet despite their obvious strength.

His torso remained vaguely human in shape but elongated, stretching like clay pulled by invisible hands. Pale flesh was now flecked with patches of black chitin, creating a mosaic of skin and insect armor.

His human hands changed as well. The fingers stretched, joints popping audibly as they extended beyond human proportion. Long black talons emerged from his fingertips with the sound of bone piercing flesh, curved like sickles and wickedly sharp. When he flexed them, they caught the light in cruel crescents.

But it was his face that completed the transformation. That too-wide grin split farther, the corners of his mouth extending beyond all human capability. From within that terrible rift, two mandibles emerged—great insectoid mouthparts that clicked and rubbed together with the sound of bone grinding against bone. They moved independently of his human mouth, creating that infernal chittering as they tasted my fear despite my best efforts to conceal it.

The cluster of additional eyes along his face now made perfect sense—a hunting design. They tracked my smallest movements while his mandibles continued their hypnotic dance. I understood, then, that I was no longer looking at something even pretending to be human.

This was Ysu in his true form—ancient, demonic, and ruled by the hunger that consumed him.

My body froze despite every instinct screaming at me to run, to flee this grove of bones and silver webs, to return to the familiar horrors of human cruelty rather than face this embodiment of otherworldly hunger. I wasn't held by any supernatural compulsion but by the simple understanding that if I ran, I would have risked everything for nothing.

I *would* have my revenge, and no demon would steal that from me.

I had sought him out. I had called his name.

And now, surrounded by the remains of those who had come before me, I finally understood the true price of the bargain I was so desperate to make.

The grove held its breath as Ysu moved over me, eight legs carrying him with unnatural ease. The luminous webs above pulsed in rhythm with his movements, as if the entire space bent to his will.

"Last chance, little human," he said, and his voice had changed too—layered now with harmonics that shouldn't coexist in a single throat. His mandibles clicked punctuation to his words. "Run back to your heated halls. Tell them you found nothing but shadows and old bones."

One of his spider legs lifted and pushed the hair out of my face. In the sharp tip, I saw my own terrified reflection multiplied in its polished surface.

"They'll hurt you for failing," he continued, circling me now, his massive form moving with impossible silence. "But their pain is known, quantifiable. What I offer..." The chittering grew louder, hungrier. "What I offer has no human words."

I lifted my chin, meeting those multiple eyes with courage I didn't feel, relying instead on the fire inside me that wanted to see it all burned to the ground. "I didn't come here to run."

"No?" All eight eyes blinked in sequence down his transformed face. "Then what did you come for?"

Before I could answer, he moved. One moment he was circling me like a cat with a mouse, and the next his human arms had seized my shoulders while his spider appendages wove around my body, lifting me from the ground as easily as a child lifts a doll. Those inhuman limbs were surprisingly cold against my skin, hard and smooth as polished stone.

He brought me level with his face, close enough that I could smell something sweet and corrupt on his breath—like flowers rotting in summer heat. His mandibles spread wide, revealing the human mouth behind them, and for a moment I glimpsed rows of teeth that belonged to neither man nor spider.

"I can taste your pain," he whispered, and one mandible brushed my cheek with terrifying gentleness. "Years of it, soaked into your very bones. Such exquisite suffering. Such carefully cultivated despair." His grip tightened, spider legs adjusting to hold me more securely. "But also...something more."

He paused, mandibles testing my skin, tasting me. The horribly light sensation of them passing over my flesh was agonizing, yet he observed me with no reaction at all—only interest.

"But perhaps I will just devour you. It has been so long since something so delicious has wandered into my web. And I am so very hungry." He wanted me to beg, to squirm in his grasp.

My mother's warnings echoed in my mind—*guard your sorrow, maiden fair*. I would, and I would *never* beg again.

"Do it," I breathed, surprising myself with the steadiness of my voice. "Whatever you're going to do, do it. I'm tired of waiting for the next horror. But promise me you will destroy them."

Something shifted in his expression—a flicker of what might have been surprise, or perhaps approval. Then his head tilted back, mandibles spreading impossibly wide, and I saw the glistening sacs at their base, swollen with venom that caught the web-light like liquid moonstone.

"As you wish, little human."

The strike was swift. His fangs pierced the soft flesh where neck meets shoulder, twin points of agony that made Gaius' careful knife work seem like gentle kisses. But the pain lasted only a heartbeat before the venom began its work.

Fire raced through my veins, but it was a cold fire—burning and freezing simultaneously. My vision fractured into prismatic shards, each showing a different version of reality. In one, I saw myself as Ysu must see me—a small, broken thing leaking pain like perfume. In another, I glimpsed something else, something with scales beneath its skin and hunger in its belly.

The venom flooded deeper, and with it came visions that weren't my own. Ancient forests spread across the land. Stone circles rose beneath stars that had different names. Blood spilled on altars while thirteen voices chanted in languages that echoed in the heart of the deep forest. Deep within me, something dark and hungry began to uncoil. And through it all, a presence—watching, waiting, weaving its vengeance across centuries.

My body convulsed in his grip, muscles seizing as the venom rewrote something fundamental in my flesh. I tried to scream, but what emerged was a sound I'd never made before—a long, harsh hiss.

He chittered in what might have been laughter. "Such strength for one so small."

The world tilted, colors bleeding into impossible spectrums. I felt my consciousness fracturing, and the last thing I saw clearly was his face above mine, fangs still dripping with venom, his expression one of terrible satisfaction.

"Sleep now, little human," he crooned as darkness rushed up to claim me. "I can't wait to devour you."

CHAPTER 5

YSU

Her pale limbs were caught in my silk, hanging like a broken doll. The threads cradled her with a tenderness I had not intended—my web responding to her as if she were something precious rather than merely prey.

Interesting.

The word surfaced in my consciousness unbidden as I observed her continued breathing. Hours had passed since I sank my fangs into the tender flesh of her throat, pumping her full of enough venom to fell a bull. By now, her life force should have been flowing through my silk, sustaining me as countless others had before.

Instead, she breathed with stubborn persistence.

I'd toyed with her. I couldn't resist. It had been so long since something as tender as her had wandered into my domain, and the hunger within me never slept. I had intended to consume her from the moment I sensed her at the edge of my web. But she had surprised me with her bravery. I hadn't known humans still possessed it in such quantities. Then again, perhaps she was merely more desperate than I'd accounted for.

It was intriguing, either way.

How long had it been since something unexpected crossed my path? Decades? A century? The new humans from the south brought their rigid roads and ordered settlements, their predictable patterns of expansion and conquest. Even their cruelties followed templates—crucifixions and systematic torture performed with the tedious efficiency of bureaucracy. Where once warriors came seeking glory in single combat, now only cowering servants fled through my domain, carrying messages between their stone fortresses.

The Romans. They had drained the mystery from this land like water from a marsh.

I circled the web, each of my eight legs finding purchase on the anchor strands without so much as a whisper. My eyes tracked every detail of her suspended form. The way her moon-pale hair cascaded through my silk—the color eerily similar. Her torn clothing sagged to reveal the constellation of scars that mapped her torment across skin that should have been flawless.

Beautiful, in the way broken things sometimes were.

The thought irritated me. Beauty was irrelevant. I was hunger incarnate, desire stripped of sentiment. I did not pause to admire my prey any more than a wolf contemplated the elegance of a deer before the kill.

And yet...

I extended one clawed finger and traced the skin above the burn scar on her shoulder, careful not to touch the web and disturb her precarious rest. The mark was fresh enough that I could almost smell the heated metal that made it; could imagine the sound of her flesh sizzling as her tormentor pressed their brand against her skin. Such deliberate artistry in her marking. The burns spoke of malice applied with patience, the cuts arranged in patterns that suggested aesthetic consideration alongside cruelty.

At least some humans retained imagination in their darker pursuits.

My eyes tracked every detail as I adjusted my position for better observation. The way her chest rose and fell. The slight flutter of her pulse at her throat. The faint scent that clung to her skin—something wild and green, like herbs crushed underfoot or smoke from sacred fires.

That scent...it stirred memories worn smooth by centuries. Priestesses who once walked these woods, women who knew the proper words to speak when darkness fell and ancient things stirred. They carried that same green fragrance, the same otherworldly quality that marked them as bridges between realms.

Bloodline. Of course.

She carried the old heritage, however diluted by generations of human breeding. I should have known. She knew my ancient name, after all. A daughter many generations removed from the priestesses who transformed me into what I am. A strange game played by fate—that she now found herself trapped in my web.

My venom could not claim her because she was protected by those who placed this curse upon me. But even the ancient bloodline should not have been enough. No, I saw the true reason when I held her in my arms and she challenged me. Rage, a fire burning so deep and hot she simply refused to die. Admirable...for a human. If my venom did not kill her, she would be a different creature when she awoke.

The prospect should have left me indifferent. Transformation was simply another form of consumption, after all. The old must die for the new to be reborn. Yet I found myself descending to her level, my legs adjusting the web's tension to bring us face-to-face. This close, I could observe the beauty of her features, the softness of her form. Qualities that stirred something deep inside me—a different kind of hunger.

When had I last witnessed such metamorphosis? When had anything in my domain surprised me with change, rather than merely feeding the eternal sameness of my hunger?

She shifted in the web, and the movement sent vibrations through every strand. My mind registered each tremor, alert in a way I had not been in longer than I cared to remember. Her body twitched violently, and I thought perhaps she had at last succumbed to my venom.

"Stop...it's too hot...you're hurting me..."

I paused as she whimpered. No—not my venom, but a nightmare. I gazed at the wound on her shoulder. Even after I revealed my true form, it was her old tormentor who haunted her dreams.

Indifference warred with something I refused to name. I had walked alone for so long that the concept of sharing my existence seemed as foreign as those Roman roads that scarred the landscape. To hope for change, for something beyond the endless cycle of hunt and wait and feed—something beyond this curse that held me stagnant—would be to invite disappointment as keen as any blade.

Better to observe, to see what she proved herself to be.

Yet as I settled myself in the web's center to wait, my multiple eyes fixed on her sleeping form, I could not entirely suppress the thought that she might wake as something genuinely new. Not merely prey marked for consumption, not another sacrifice to sustain my immortal appetite, but something...more.

The web trembled as she twitched in sleep, and my silk

responded to her as if she were already part of my domain, already transforming into something that might—if I permitted such foolish speculation—stand beside me rather than cower beneath me.

I watched her dream. When she woke, we would see what manner of creature emerged from this chrysalis of venom and inherited power.

And perhaps—though I guarded the thought—perhaps the long solitude that had defined my existence since my curse was placed upon me might finally find interruption.

But I was careful not to hope. Hope, after all, was a luxury monsters like myself could rarely afford.

CHAPTER 6

FLAVIA

As my consciousness returned, everything narrowed to the intense tingling in my limbs.

The sensation spread through my hands, racing up my arms with a peculiar mixture of numbness and hypersensitivity that made me wonder if I still possessed flesh at all. My fingertips felt swollen, as if a thousand needles danced across their surface.

I tried to flex them and failed miserably.

My eyes snapped open to a world washed in shadows. I hung suspended in his web. The silk cradled my body, supporting my weight while binding me as surely as iron chains.

Every breath sent tremors through the web's geometry, and I felt the vibrations echo across the grove. The threads pressed against my skin, and when I struggled against them, they seemed to tighten in response.

Panic clawed at my throat as I tested my bonds more urgently. My left arm was caught at an awkward angle, wrapped in silk from wrist to shoulder. My legs were equally contained, ankles bound together. When I twisted my torso, searching for leverage, the web rocked gently, stretching without releasing its grip.

The tingling in my fingers intensified, spreading to my toes, my lips, the sensitive skin of my neck. It felt like awakening from deep sleep, but magnified tenfold—as if every nerve in my body had been dormant and was now stirring to painful, vibrant life.

"Ah," came a voice from the darkness beyond the web's luminous aura. "So you have awakened."

I stopped struggling, turning toward the sound. Ysu emerged from the shadows. He appeared human again, his additional spider-like arms concealed beneath his dark robe. Only his eyes betrayed his true nature, all eight tracking my every movement.

"Let me down." My voice came out rough, scraped raw by whatever poison he'd pumped into my veins.

"In time." He circled the web slowly, studying me the way I'm sure he studied any other prey in his clutches. "First, we must establish certain...understandings."

The silk pressed against my skin like dozens of gentle fingers and I fought the urge to struggle again. Instead, I met his gaze directly, drawing on reserves of defiance bolstered by the fact that he hadn't decided to kill me after all.

"You claimed you would be my bride," he continued, his tone conversational. "That bargain comes with obligations. Duties."

Without ceremony, one of his concealed limbs sliced through the strands holding me aloft. I dropped to the forest floor in an ungraceful heap, silk threads clinging to me, whispering against my skin as they floated on the night's cool breeze. Before I could fully regain my footing, his human hand grasped my arm and pulled me upright.

"Come," he said, already moving deeper into the grove. "There is a spring not far from here where you will bathe me, as befits a bride attending her husband."

I planted my feet, resisting his tug. It was a small force, one he could have easily overcome. Instead, he stopped and turned back to me, all his dark eyes fixed on me.

"Has my venom caused you to forget our bargain, little human?" His other hand traced up my neck until he grasped my chin between his thumb and forefinger. "You are mine. You will obey." His thumb dragged over my lower lip, tugging slightly. "Or do you no longer desire your revenge?"

I did not flinch. I would not flinch. "I desire it."

"Then obey." He flicked his thumb away, and his sharp nail cut my lip. I did not wince. I merely extended my tongue to lap up the hot bubble of metallic blood that welled there. All eight of his eyes followed the movement with an intensity I could feel.

I nodded.

He turned away, confident I would follow without further resistance. I hesitated only a moment before trailing after him, out of his grove of horrors.

The forest beyond his web was unlike anything that existed in the daylight world. Ancient trees leaned inward, their branches interwoven in patterns that spoke of centuries of patient growth guided by inhuman intelligence. Moss climbed their trunks in spirals, and where my bare feet touched the earth, I felt a thrumming beneath the surface—as if the land itself pulsed with some vast, sleeping heartbeat.

Ysu moved ahead of me, his robe billowing behind him

despite the absence of wind. The fabric drank in the moonlight, creating the illusion that he was part of the darkness itself. Occasionally, I caught glimpses of movement beneath the cloth—the subtle shift of his concealed limbs, inhuman joints twitching.

The tingling in my fingers had spread throughout my body now, a constant whisper that made every sensation more acute. It must have been a lingering effect of his venom. The rough bark of the trees my feet brushed against felt sharper than shattered glass. The cool night air caressed me until every inch of my skin felt raw and exposed.

But it wasn't just my skin. The fragrance of night-blooming flowers carried undertones of sweetness I had never noticed before. It felt misplaced in this place of death. I heard the soft calls of animals much farther into the forest than I would have thought possible.

We walked a quarter mile through this twilight realm before the sound reached us—water moving over stone. The spring emerged from the forest, a natural pool ten feet across, fed by water that seeped between moss-covered rocks.

The water glowed. Not with reflected moonlight, but with its own inner radiance, as if each drop carried a fragment of a captured star. Steam rose from its surface into the cool night air, and where the water met the pool's edges, small flowers bloomed in impossible colors—blues that verged on silver, purples that edged toward black. Vines crawled up the surrounding trees, bearing huge trumpet-like white blossoms that opened under the moonlight. I had never seen anything like this before, and suspected such beauty could only exist because of the pool's warmth.

Ysu stopped at the pool's rim and turned to face me, his multiple eyes reflecting the water's ethereal light. Then he turned back to the spring, and without ceremony or modesty, unfastened whatever hidden clasps held his robe in place. The fabric fell away, revealing the full expanse of his bare back. The additional arms that emerged from along his spine, midway down, entranced me—the chitin there slowly morphing into black skin. As he moved, I could see the power of every muscle.

Despite his monstrous appetite, he wasn't soft like so many Roman centurions. Every inch of him was carved like the statues in the villa foyer, though he was so much larger—as if every one of his victims had been absorbed to supplement his strength.

I was so entranced by the shape of him that I hardly noticed when he loosened the cloth at his waist, letting it sag. A gasp nearly escaped me as the full, naked expanse of his muscular ass was revealed—just as sculpted as the rest of him. Male nudity had, until this point, only brought me fear, knowing the consequences it carried. But seeing him, something so beyond human while still being so perfectly formed, sent a foreign sensation coiling low in my belly. It felt like a serpent curled beneath my skin, hungry and waiting.

He stepped into the pool, the glowing water accepting him as if this place had been carved from the earth specifically for his use. The spring reached his waist, and steam rose around him like incense offered to a forgotten god.

When he settled himself against the far side of the pool, he raised a human hand and beckoned me forward with one crooked finger—a gesture that managed to be both invitation and command.

"Come," he said simply. "Join me."

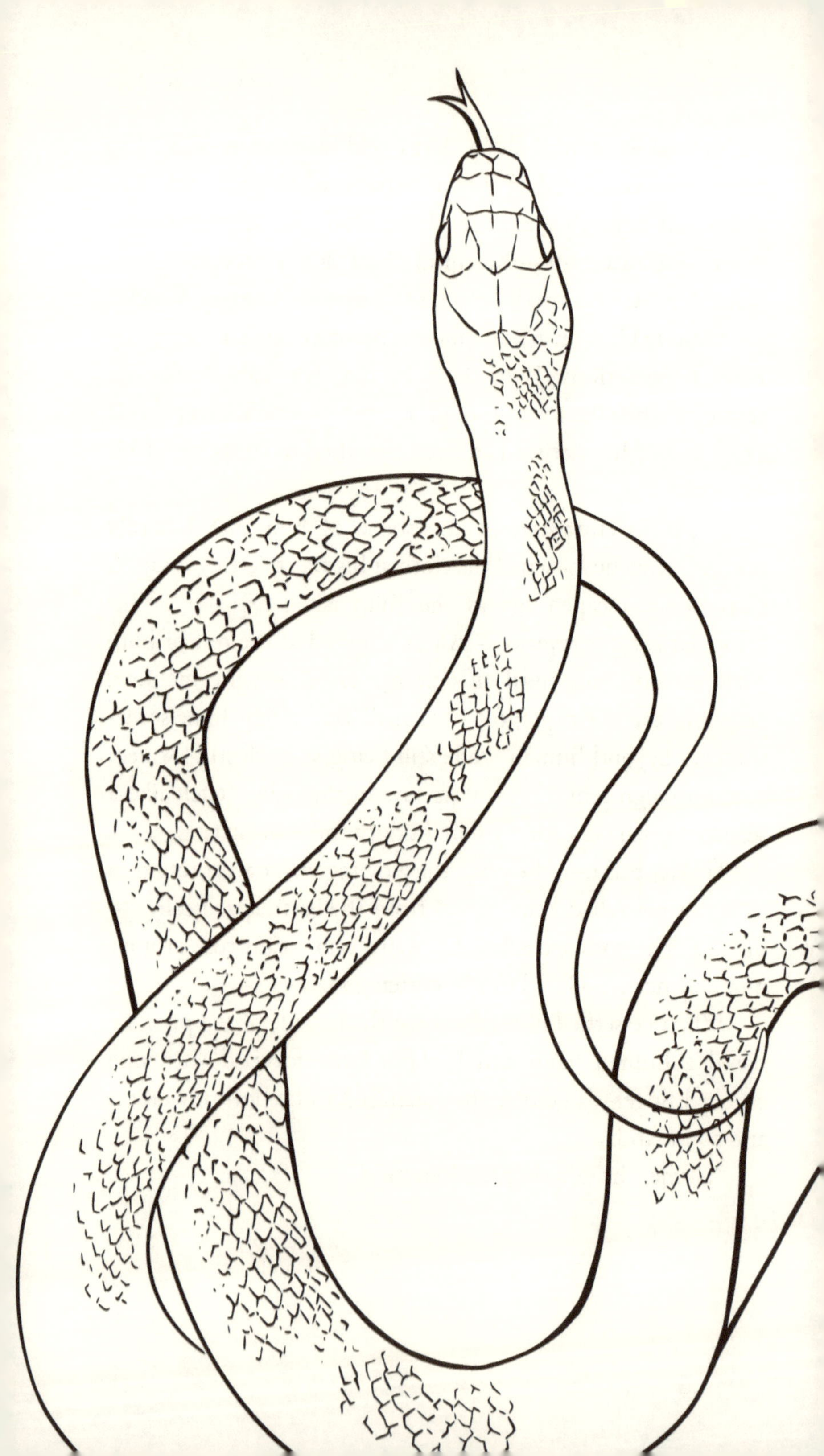

CHAPTER 7

FLAVIA

His four spider arms spread along the bank of the spring—unmoving, almost blending in with the rocks and detritus of the forest floor. But I had long ago learned what a predator lying in wait looked like.

"Little human..." The warning in his voice was clear. I scrambled over and kneeled just behind him at the edge. It likely wasn't what he intended, but it was a skill that had always served me well distracting Tiberius' men. I placed my hands on the flesh of his massive shoulders.

"What are you—" he began, but when I pressed my thumbs into the crevice where his muscles met, he stilled.

He was tight, but I felt his muscles relax just as a man's would under my ministrations. I don't know what I expected from a demon, but his anatomy wasn't so different from the other men—just larger. At least near his neck and human arms. I pressed my thumbs into the column of muscle and tendons that ran up the back of his neck, then spread my nails over the skin beneath his long, dark hair.

He let out a low, reverberating chuckle. "Are you trying to distract me?"

"Does this not please you?"

"Clever little thing," he murmured, his voice carrying amusement and something darker. "You think to disarm me with touch?"

"It worked on lesser predators." I dug my thumbs deeper into the knots of tension, feeling the way his breathing shifted. I traced my hands lower, closer to where his inhuman arms emerged. The skin there was rougher than leather armor, darkening into something closer to black iron where his segmented limbs broke through. It should have disturbed me, his monstrous anatomy. Instead, I gently scraped my nails over the rough texture in fascination. "Though perhaps you're more resilient than Roman dogs."

"How flattering. Comparing me to your former tormentors." His tone remained irreverent, but I caught the edge beneath it. "Tell me, did they purr like house cats when you touched them this way?"

My hands stilled. "No. They took what they wanted. I merely survived."

"Survived," he repeated slowly. "Such an interesting word choice. Not submitted. Not surrendered." One of his additional eyes swiveled to watch my face, searching for a reaction. I gave him none. His too-wide mouth dipped into a frown.

The rough, shell-like texture of one of his arms wrapped around my waist, and in the next moment I was drowning in heat. Hot water surrounded me and I was back in that villa, my body pressed against those heated floors—floors far too warm for comfort—as knives and heated pokers tore apart my skin again and again.

Bursting out of the water, I heaved as I coughed liquid

from my lungs. I coughed again and shook my head, water streaming from my hair as I scrambled backward toward the spring's edge, my torn stola clinging to me like a second skin. I clung to the rocks but shook too badly to pull myself out.

"No, no, no," I gasped, the words tumbling out between ragged breaths. The heat—it was everywhere, seeping through my clothes, into my pores, reminding me of those terrible nights when they dragged me down to the basement where the floors burned like the fires of Dis itself.

Ysu remained perfectly still in the water, his multiple eyes fixed on me with an expression I couldn't read. Steam rose around him, but he made no move to approach, no gesture of comfort or threat. He simply...observed.

"Curious," he said finally, his voice carrying that irritatingly detached interest. "You showed no such reaction to my form, to my venom, to the prospect of death itself. Yet heated water reduces you to this?"

I managed to stand and wrapped my arms around myself, shivering violently despite the warmth that still submerged me.

"I have endured much," I managed, trying to regain some semblance of composure. "But heat...heat brings back things I would rather forget."

His head tilted slightly, a gesture that might have been almost human if not for the way his additional eyes moved independently, studying me

"Ah. The Romans and their love of heated baths and floors. How they wish to drive away the cold that defines these lands."

It wasn't a question, but I nodded anyway.

"Fascinating. Warmth—something most of your kind finds comforting—sends you into panic."

"Perhaps I'm broken," I said bitterly.

"Too demanding to be broken," he replied, a hint of

amusement threading through his tone. "Perhaps you simply see the honesty in the cold and darkness."

No response came to me, so I bit my lip and looked anywhere but at those eight lingering eyes.

"Show me," he said suddenly, his voice carrying new authority. "Disrobe. I would see the full extent of what they have done to you."

I stiffened. "I will not—"

"You will." His tone brooked no argument, though he still made no move to approach me. "You are my bride now, bound to me by bargain and venom. I have claimed you, and I would know exactly what condition my prize is in."

The word *prize* stung, but I forced myself to meet his gaze. "You wish to catalog my damage like some merchant examining livestock?"

"Livestock?" His laugh was dark, genuinely amused. "Little human, livestock is raised for slaughter. You, I intend to keep."

The possessiveness in his voice did not affect me as Tiberius' had, even as I bristled at his presumption. Tiberius had thought me a possession, his amusing toy. Something in Ysu's unnatural stare told me a different story.

"And if I refuse?"

"Then you refuse." He shrugged, the gesture oddly casual for a creature of his size. "I am patient, and I have time. Perhaps an eternity of it. But you are the one whose heart burns with a desire for revenge. How much time do you have?"

No time at all. I wanted them all dead, and I wanted it now. The thought of them enjoying another day, unburdened by the pain they caused was unbearable. I was gone, but another would take my place. They might have already found my replacement.

His expression gave away nothing, just the same appraising stare.

"If you uphold our bargain, make no mistake—I will see all of you eventually. The question is how quickly you wish to succumb to me," he said, and his neutral face broke into a maddening grin.

"How gracious of you to give me the illusion of control." I crossed my arms over my chest, as if that would hide me from him.

"Illusion?" His smile widened past the point where he looked human, his fangs flashing in the moonlight. Faster than I could track, one of his spider arms lashed out. I felt it pass over my arm and braced for pain.

There was none.

Instead, one sleeve of my poor, tortured stola fell away, sliced cleanly without so much as grazing my skin.

I watched it float in the pool for a moment before returning to his gaze. The message was clear.

"My dear bride, if I wanted you naked, you would be naked. If I wanted you spread beneath me, you would be trembling and begging for more. The fact that you're still clothed and defiant should tell you something about the nature of control here."

Heat flushed through me at his words—not the painful heat of memory, but something else entirely. "You're quite confident for a creature who's been alone in these woods for three centuries."

"Three centuries of hunting, little human. Three centuries of learning exactly how the human body works." His smile grew even more wicked, if such a thing was possible. "Testing exactly what will make you scream."

The shiver that ran down my spine wasn't from fear, and he knew it.

"I wish to understand what manner of creature I have bound myself to," he continued with that same maddening calm. "Your scars tell stories. They speak of endurance, of survival, of a will that would not break despite every effort to shatter it. These are not shameful marks."

His words caught me off guard. In all my years of torment, no one had ever suggested that my survival was anything other than cowardice, that my scars were anything other than proof of weakness. Tiberius had marked my entire body, but he had always kept my face unmarred. He still wanted to show me off whenever the centurions came through for visits—his golden barbarian wife they could all covet. Then he would reveal my true nature to them, and they would sneer with disgust as they fucked me.

Ysu would do the same.

Perhaps my thoughts showed on my face, because I could have sworn his gaze softened—though it might have been a trick of the light rising from the pool. "Little human, I am a creature born of curse and shadow, transformed by ancient magic into something that hunts in the darkness. Do you truly think the marks left by mortal cruelty would disturb me?"

"No," I said slowly, realization dawning. "You'd probably find them...useful. Like a map to every weakness."

"So distrustful, my bride." His approval was evident, though it carried a dangerous edge. "I suspect your weaknesses are not where your scars lie. Those marks represent places where you refused to break. Your true vulnerabilities..." His gaze traveled over me assessingly. "Those likely remain...untouched."

I stood slowly, water dripping from my soaked clothing.

The tingling in my extremities had spread into a deep humming throughout my entire body, and I found that his presence—his attention—calmed the thrum in my blood. As if his venom sensed its master.

"You want to see my scars so badly?" I asked, fingers moving to the clasp of my torn stola. "What will you give me in return?"

He raised an eyebrow. "Bold. Still negotiating with a demon while half drowned and trembling."

"Survival." It was all I said, but he understood.

"And what would you ask of me?"

I considered, then smiled with more confidence than I felt. *Never let them see you falter.* "A truth. Something you've never told another soul."

"A high price." But he looked intrigued. "What husband would refuse his bride? Very well—show me your scars, and I'll show you mine."

With trembling fingers, I released the clasp. The wet fabric slid from my shoulders, landing with a wet thud on the surface of the spring. All his eyes stilled, focusing on me. His hard claws pressed against my back as he coaxed me forward between his submerged legs.

His hands reached out, tracing the numerous cuts along my arms and the particularly large burn beside my belly button. His hands were huge, his fingers spreading so wide they could cover my entire stomach, but he moved them softly, the black skin that transitioned into long nails gliding like a painter's brush over a canvas. I hadn't experienced touch this gentle since I was a child—when I was still cherished and loved.

"Your former husband did all this to you? He truly was a master of cruelty." He said it without inflection, just another observation.

"Him...and his men." As I spoke, I felt the smallest hesitation in his hand.

"He let someone else touch what was his?" For the first time, I saw disgust on his face. "Men truly are such fools. I will not allow such blasphemy."

"Possessive creature," I murmured, though his words sent an unexpected thrill through me.

"When I claim something, I keep it." His fingers traced along my collarbone. "Unmarked by others. Protected."

Goosebumps rose across my skin as his fingers continued their exploration, their size stark against my body. Why did that excite me? Because I knew how easily he would destroy the Romans. That was the reason...no other.

"And my truth?" I asked, even as his touch made my breath catch.

His hand stilled, all his eyes fixing on mine. For a long moment, he seemed to weigh whether to answer at all.

"I was not always bound to these woods," he said finally, his voice quieter than I'd ever heard it. "Before the curse, I chose my prey. I decided when to hunt, when to conquer, when to kill, when to spare. The transformation...it took that from me."

I studied his face, seeing something almost vulnerable in the way his additional eyes had stopped their constant movement. "What do you mean?"

"The hunger is not truly mine. It belongs to the curse, driving me to feed whether I wish to or not. For three centuries, I have been little more than a trap set by ancient magic, snaring whatever stumbles into my domain, into this forest." His claws traced a gentle path along my ribs. "But you...for the first time in three hundred years, I wanted something beyond mere sustenance. I was able to resist the hunger."

The confession hit me unexpectedly. I had assumed he was simply a predator following his nature, but this...this suggested a creature enslaved to forces he could not control.

"So the great Devourer has desires beyond hunger?" I murmured. "How unexpectedly...human of you."

His laugh was bitter. "It appears so. You have awakened a part of me I thought long ago consumed by the void within me."

His fingers traced up and over the swell of my breast. I might have mistaken it for the same clinical touch as before, except he circled the pad of his thumb around my nipple until it hardened. That overly wide smirk returned.

"Your body still recognizes pleasure, little human. This is—"

"I have a name, you know," I interrupted.

His hand stilled, all his eyes fixing on mine. "Yes, a name given to you by those human invaders. Those who have desecrated these lands, and desecrated you. Wouldn't you prefer a name that echoes with the wisdom of your ancestors, that resonates with the soul of this land?"

I froze in his grasp. "How did you know my mother was Briton?"

He wound a lock of my silver hair around his finger, sliding it up until I felt his claws gliding over the back of my head. Then, with a harsh jolt, he tugged me against his chest, his cheek brushing mine as his lips grazed the shell of my ear.

"I can taste it in you, smell it. They tried to burn it out of you, but your blood smells of moss-covered forests and night-blooming flowers. You smell like these woods—an ancientness slumbering, waiting to arise again."

His tongue snaked along my jaw, and I shivered as he spread his fingers over my lower back, pulling me closer. As my bare sex collided with him, there was no doubt I had awakened something within him, and it felt hard and terrifyingly large.

"I'm going to give you one last chance. You have seen what I really am and survived. Never before have I let prey leave this grove alive, but you...intrigue me. Say you wish to flee, and I will allow it."

His grip didn't loosen. "But if you still desire that revenge that burns in your heart so bright it burned away my poison, it's time to test how brave you truly are."

He dipped his head, and that impossibly long tongue wrapped around my breast, the heat of it a sharp contrast to his cold hands, and I trembled. It reminded me of pain and hot irons. He pulled back and blew over the wet skin, the cold sensation enough to make it draw tight, and the smallest groan escaped me.

"Know this, my bride—if you stay, you are mine. This pretty little body of yours is mine, and I intend to use it. Every whimper you make, every time your legs shake and you seize with more pleasure than you think you can handle, it will only prove exactly how much you belong to me."

"Such promises," I breathed, embolden by bravado and the unfamiliar sensation coiling low in my belly. "I hope you can deliver on them."

His eyes flashed dangerously. "Careful. You might get exactly what you're asking for."

The words rose out of me, born from the fire his venom had stoked inside me. "I'm counting on it."

His eyes went entirely black. "I will devour you until the delicious nectar of your ecstasy fills this endless void of hunger within me. But you must choose to stay. There can only be pleasure if it's shared."

He was giving me a choice. Something I'd never had before.

Something that had been taken away from him. I could run, try to find a new home—perhaps among one of the tribes still rumored to survive to the north. But if I did that, Tiberius and his men would live, and I would never be free. I had made my choice while bleeding on the tiled villa floor, and I would not turn back now.

And the truth was, with all his arms wrapped around me and his broad chest pressed against mine, I wanted to know exactly what lay hidden beneath the spring's surface.

"We have a deal, don't we?"

He hummed with satisfaction and pushed me away from him.

He rose from the spring, and my mouth fell open. What emerged from the water was not one hard cock but two, each bobbing slightly with his movement. He laughed as I tried to school my face into something other than shock.

"Scared, little human?"

For the first time in my memory, I wasn't. Instead, the serpent in my belly writhed, and my mouth watered as she drove me closer to him. I reached out, one hand to each of his lengths. The upper shaft was slightly smaller than the one below, yet both pulsed with thick veins a shade darker than the surrounding grayish skin. I traced my thumb along the dark, prominent vein that curved down the side of his larger cock until it twitched.

The serpent beneath my skin uncoiled further as I stroked him, marveling at the smooth texture, like silk over iron. His breath hitched, and for the first time since entering his domain, I felt the power shift—not merely flowing from him to me, but circulating like the strange currents in the glowing pool.

"Brave little human," he murmured, his many eyes tracking my movements with an intensity that should have terrified me.

Instead, a newfound hunger rose. "Do you know what you're doing?"

"No," I admitted, my voice steadier than I expected. "But I'm a fast learner."

I leaned forward, mouth open, guiding him toward me, aching to devour him.

His laugh rumbled through the grove, setting the leaves trembling. In one fluid motion he lifted me from the water, armored arms cradling me against his chest while his human hands roamed my scarred skin. Each touch left trails of tingling fire—his venom singing in my veins, awakening nerves I'd thought long dead.

"Patience," he whispered. "You are mine now, and you taste so sweet. There are so many ways I look forward to devouring you."

Moss cushioned our descent; above us, his web shimmered, droplets of moisture catching moonlight like scattered stars.

"Let me show you what it can feel like," he breathed against my ear, one claw gliding over the curve of my hip, "even after all they did to bury it beneath pain."

His tongue—impossibly long, impossibly hot—laved the scars along my ribs. I arched beneath him, a raw sound tearing free that I didn't recognize as my own. Not a scream. Not a plea. Something new.

I covered my mouth, an old reflex.

All his eyes lifted to mine, anger flaring in their depths. "You are *mine,* including all those pretty sounds you make. Don't you dare hold them back. They belong to me now."

I had always forced myself to stay silent in the villa, my cries only ever bringing more pain. I'd bitten my tongue, praying for it to end. But I didn't want this to end. I wanted more.

I nodded, and he lowered his head between my legs. His

tongue swept over the sensitive skin of my inner thigh, then slipped slowly between my folds and deep inside me. My hips bucked at the sensation, and I let my moan rise unhindered into the night. It wasn't harsh or painful—only soft, impossibly deep, a pressure unlike anything I'd ever known.

"That's it," he crooned, the sound laced with satisfied clicks. "Remember what it means to be more than prey."

Without thought, I raked my hands through his dark hair as his tongue continued moving over me. He alternated between pressing deep inside me and swirling that long muscle along my lips and around my clit, each pass firmer, until I was panting—one step closer to the release my body had craved for months, a release I'd been too broken to reach.

"Ysu..." His name tore from my lips as my hips bucked against his face.

His hand slid down my inner thigh, and I cried out when he plunged one enormous finger into me, lifting his head.

"You cry my name, yet I'm not sure if it's curse or prayer, invocation or damnation. Either way, I will devour you."

He lowered his head again and sucked my clit into his mouth with such force my back arched off the soft moss. He continued that steady, ruthless rhythm, the finger inside me curling as a deep throbbing built. He worked me open slowly, patiently, before I felt the incredible stretch as he added another. Another cry of pleasure ripped free, and I saw nothing but moonlight glittering on his web overhead as he drove me over the edge.

I shattered—every muscle seizing, not with terror but with pure elation. Waves of pleasure rolled through me, Ysu never ceasing his ministrations, guiding me through them until I was entirely spent.

It was unlike any release I'd ever had. Deeper and shared.

Not stolen in the dark but blazing open under the moonlight while all his eyes drank me in with rapture.

When he had wrung the very last tremor from me, he rose and moved his massive body over mine.

"You're trembling, little human. Are you scared..." His fangs grazed the skin over my pulse. "Or is my little blood-thirsty bride excited by the thought of being consumed by the darkness?" His tongue, still unbearably warm, pressed against my neck until I could feel my heartbeat pulsing beneath it. "Or perhaps you like the thought that I could tear you apart without a second thought—but instead choose to worship you until you're falling apart?"

I didn't answer—couldn't—my heart still pounding in my chest.

He pulled back, and his face split into that too-wide smile. "I hope you're not done yet. Not when you're finally ready for me. We're just getting started."

Four arms snaked under my body and lifted me as he shifted. He settled back against the stones at the edge of the pond, spreading his legs and depositing me so I straddled him, caught between his two cocks. One rubbed over my still-sensitive clit while the other nestled between my ass cheeks. Precum smeared across my stomach as he rocked against me—thicker than any I had experienced before, the broad head nearly reaching my belly button as he painted me with it.

His too-large hands wrapped completely around my waist and hips, raising me just enough that both cocks notched at my entrance. Memories of pain flickered, but I would not hesitate, not now. I started to sink down, only for his grip to tighten, stilling me.

"I appreciate your eagerness, little human, but I do not intend to break you so soon." All eight of his eyes sparkled with wickedness as his cockheads slid through the wetness at my core, mixing his thick fluids with mine. The smaller caught at my entrance, then glided forward to stroke my clit while the larger began to press inside.

His hand traced up my spine until he gripped the back of my neck, and his hand was so large it nearly encircled my entire throat.

He held me tight, using that grip as leverage as he drove me down onto him, my body stretching around him. The burn shifted into that same tingling that covered my skin, his venom changing something in me I didn't fully understand. Still, I clenched down, trying to resist the intrusion.

He felt my resistance and slowed, tracing his hands down my arms. His fingers pressed my clenched fists open, and my entire body relaxed unconsciously as I sank another inch onto him. He guided my hands to his chest, and I was once again reminded of how much larger he was than me. But beneath his cool, smooth skin, I felt his heart beating—much faster than I expected.

I looked up into his eyes, and all of them were watching me with such intensity that I looked away again. He gripped my chin, forcing my gaze back to his.

"You are mine. I will not allow any harm to come to you," he said. My breath caught in my throat. "I will not push you past what you can handle, but you *can* handle me, little human. In fact"—he wrapped all his arms around me, pulling me tight—"I know you can. Just try a little harder."

My legs shook from the effort of holding myself up, and he took all my weight into his arms, his serrated claws pressing into my bare skin just enough to trigger the buzzing of his venom. He lifted me until he was barely seated inside me, then slowly pushed me back down. I took him deeper, his cock filling me more than I had ever been filled before—but it still wasn't enough.

"Relax, I have you." His voice was a low hum, and I sank lower.

I was panting, the feeling of him unbearably deep. My fingers tightened on his chest, and I willed myself to open when his tongue pressed between my parted lips. I let out a sound of surprise, but he didn't stop, filling my mouth with his tongue until our lips met. It wasn't a kiss—it was a claiming—but as all his arms wrapped tighter around me and he filled every inch of me, I felt myself surrender.

I rolled my tongue back against his, and he tasted metallic, with a hint of the sweetness of overripe fruit just on the edge of decay. He let out a low groan of satisfaction as I moved my lips against his, and finally I uncoiled, letting him fill me until he pressed against the deepest part of me.

Our hips met, and he released my mouth, grinning as all eight of his eyes blinked. His hand moved back to the nape of my neck, leaning me back as his other hand traced the bulge in my stomach.

"You fit me perfectly. Perhaps fate did bring you to me."

His grip tightened, and he lifted me up and slammed me back down. I let out a cry, but it was more shock than pain. And as he continued to move, that shock and pressure transformed into something much sweeter.

His top cock slid against my clit again and again. My breasts bounced obscenely with each thrust, and my eyes rolled back as inhuman sounds tore from my lips.

"Yes—let me hear those beautiful moans while your ravenous cunt swallows my cock."

The space between us was slick with my arousal and his precum, his upper cock bobbing heavily. I wrapped my fingers around it, fisting it tight in time with his thrusts. Sinking to the base, I watched his eyes roll back, and seeing this monster lose himself in me was intoxicating in a way I had never known. I squeezed tighter, moved faster, reclaiming my legs instead of letting him use me like a rag doll. I rode him hard, keeping him pinned against my stomach as my cunt consumed him.

Another release coiled inside me, and I chased it now. I wanted it—wanted to come around his cock and milk him until he popped. Strength and stamina I didn't know I possessed surged through me, refusing to let him escape. The buzzing beneath my skin reached a feverish pitch, like something wild desperate to break free. Desperate for its prey.

All eight of his eyes found me, and a lazy grin crossed his face. "There she is."

The tingling of his venom was everywhere, but it concentrated at my core, and I was close. So, so close.

I moved faster, slamming myself onto him, until everything tightened and then released in an orgasm even more powerful than the first. The tingling spread from my center to the tips of my fingers and toes, and my whole body shook as I collapsed against his chest.

But the sensation didn't stop. He wouldn't let it. Even as my legs gave out, he rolled his hips up into me with each aftershock, holding me tight.

Everything was too much. My mouth opened wide, and then my teeth sank into the flesh of his shoulder, tasting something rich and metallic. He made a sound of approval that vibrated through us both.

"So ferocious, neidr."

I had learned some of the old language, but that word was new. Still, as his flesh yielded beneath my teeth, it felt right.

My nails—so much sharper than I remembered—raked

down his back, and he drove faster, deeper, until I felt him tense.

His tongue found my mouth, pressing to the back of my throat as I clenched around him. Hot ropes of cum spilled over my stomach and fingers while he pumped into me, finally claiming his own release.

Everything was out of focus. I heard him speaking, but the words didn't reach me. Warmth covered my skin, and a distant part of me wanted to panic again, but that part felt far away. I realized he had lowered me into the spring, cleaning me off.

The tingling that had been building since I awoke was subdued now—gentler, almost content, as though it had been satiated, at least for a time.

He wrapped my stola around me like a blanket, and I let my head rest against his cool, broad chest as he carried me back toward his web.

"You did well, neidr. Rest now," he murmured against the top of my head. "You will need your strength tomorrow."

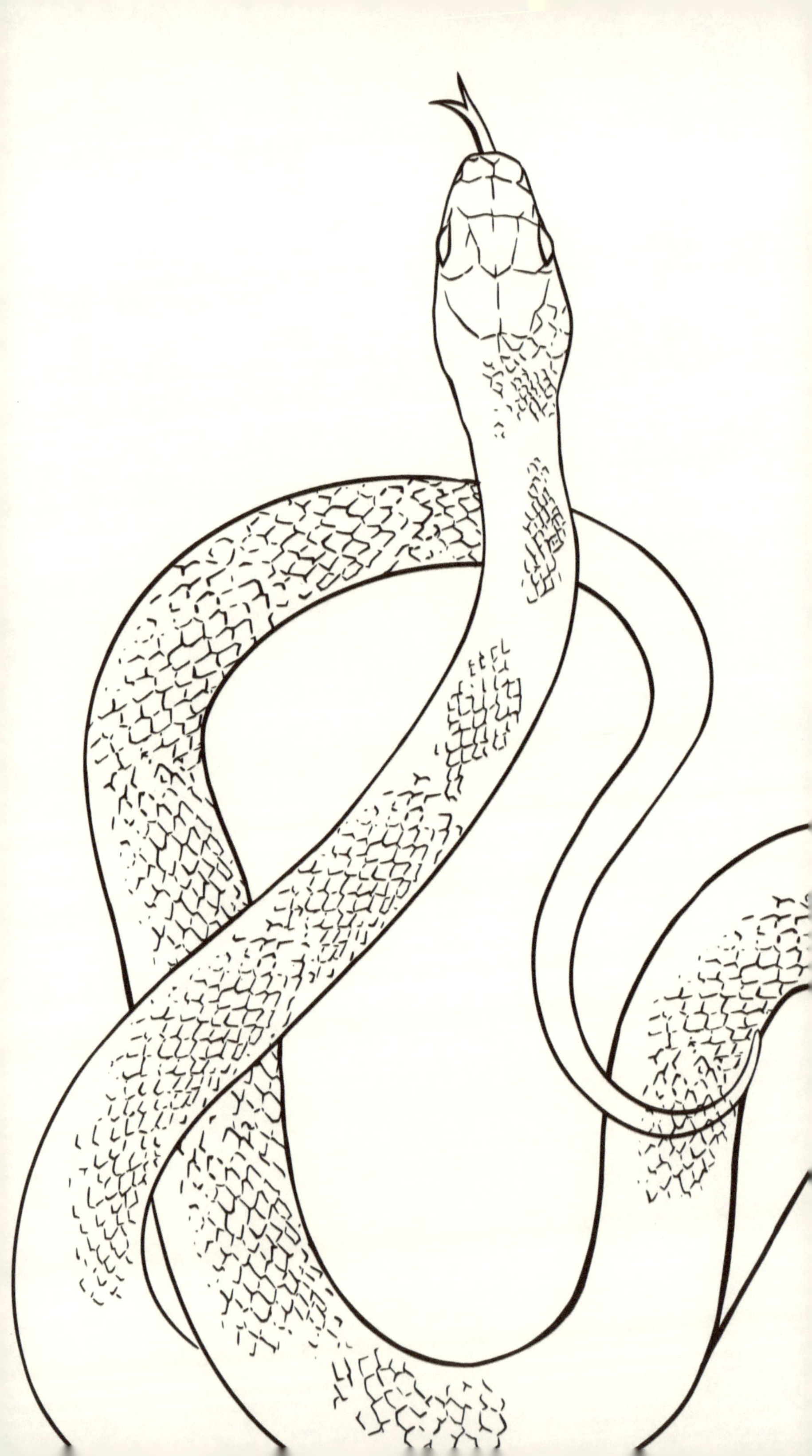

CHAPTER 8

FLAVIA

My sleep was broken by the same nightmare I'd had for years. Hands grabbing me in the darkness, laughing faces, hot metal pressed against my skin as the smell of my own singed flesh filled my nostrils. But for the first time, my wicked dreams were disturbed by someone else.

"Damn it, neidr, you're disturbing my entire web." A strong arm locked around me, pulling my back against a broad chest. But it wasn't hot or confining. I should have fought, should have tried to pry myself away, but his venom running through my veins knew its home, and it curled up, content.

Ysu shifted behind me, his spider limbs winding around us in the darkness, and I was cradled as silver threads wove around me. But it wasn't a trap or a prison, not this time. His cool fingers traced down the side of my cheek.

"Sleep. You are mine. No harm will come to you."

For some reason, I believed him. Perhaps it was the hum of his venom in my blood, or the pleasant ache from our time at the spring, but sleep found me easily.

This time, my dream was different.

The villa burned with cold fire.

I watched from above, suspended in darkness, as Ysu moved through the corridors I knew so well. His true form filled the space between floor and ceiling, eight legs carrying him soundlessly while his inhuman arms reached into rooms, plucking soldiers from their beds like grapes from a vine.

Marcus emerged from his chamber, sword raised, his familiar wine-courage making him bold. The blade passed through empty air where Ysu had been a heartbeat before. Then silk wrapped around the Roman's throat, lifting him until his feet kicked uselessly above the mosaic floors. I watched his face purple, watched recognition dawn in his eyes as he realized the nightmare that now held him in its grasp.

Screams filled the air. Gaius' high, boyish shriek cut through the night as silver threads dragged him across the heated floors he so loved to watch my blood decorate. Other soldiers rushed from their quarters, but the trap had been set. They ran into silk barriers that sliced through bronze armor like parchment, leaving them tangled and bleeding, suspended like offerings to this dark god.

Through it all, Tiberius' voice rose above the chaos, shouting orders no one could follow, demanding explanations from Roman gods who had long abandoned him. Ysu approached the wooden double doors of Tiberius' private chamber, and I heard the frantic scraping as furniture was shoved to barricade the other side. Ysu laughed—slow, cruel— like something so trivial could stop him.

He slammed his claws into the wood and the door shattered, dust filling the air as Ysu's monstrous form filled Tiberius' sanctuary. My former husband scrambled away, fleeing for the balcony.

Ysu was no longer silent. He let his claws click across the tile with deliberate slowness, his mandibles emitting that incessant chittering that echoed off the stone walls.

His claws pierced the tile around Tiberius, caging him in, and his screams filled the air as Ysu descended.

The dream shifted, and I was the web itself, strung throughout the villa's sprawling halls. I felt every vibration as my victims struggled. I tasted their terror through the silk, sweet as honeyed wine. Then I was something else, something with scales and a hunger so deep I could think of nothing else. I slid across the heated tiles toward a soldier caught in the web. He screamed, but it died out as my jaw opened impossibly wide, and—

I woke with the taste of iron in my mouth.

The grove was painted in dawn's gray light, and below me, Ysu fed. His mandibles worked methodically, piercing the torso of what had once been a man. The sound was wet and organic—flesh parting, fluids draining. The body was wrapped in silk from neck to knees, face mercifully obscured, but I recognize the bronze studs on what remained of the armor.

A villa guard. One of many complicit in my torture.

I should have felt horror. Revulsion. Fear. Instead, I watched with the same detached curiosity Ysu had shown while cataloging my scars. The darkness in my belly stirred—not with hunger exactly, but with something adjacent to it. Satisfaction at my justice served.

A thought crossed my mind. This could have been me, suspended and drained. It should have been me, but Ysu's venom had not taken root. Even knowing that, I felt no remorse for the man's fate.

"You're awake." Ysu didn't look up from his meal, but several of his eyes tracked my movement as I descended from his web. He had woven me what might have been considered a hammock, the silk less sticky so I could sleep without restraint, but still held safely. I climbed down awkwardly, feet and hands catching on various threads, making the whole web vibrate as I tugged free. Ysu shivered with the disturbance but said nothing.

The tingle that had subsided during my time with him had returned, fiercer now. It felt like the same cold fire the villa had burned with in my dream.

I approached Ysu, his victim now reduced to little more than pools of viscera on the forest floor, bones gleaming bright white in the early light.

"Did you destroy them all?" My voice was steady, but my hands shook.

He paused in his feeding, mandibles retracting as he turned to face me fully. Gore painted his mouth and body, but his smile was almost fond. "Every last one, neidr. We had a deal, didn't we?" He leaned his head down and to the side, his long tongue extending to lick the blood from his bulky shoulder muscle. I enjoyed the sight far too much, remembering exactly what that tongue had done.

"I want to see it."

His laugh rumbled through the grove, disturbing the morning birds. "Do you now? How delightfully morbid." He rose, leaving the half-consumed corpse behind. I watched as hundreds of insects rose from the forest detritus to overtake it, as though they'd been silently waiting their turn. "As it happens, I saved something special for you. A gift, one might say."

The way his multiple eyes glittered with dark amusement made my pulse quicken. "A gift?"

"Think of it as a wedding present." His mandibles chittered at his own joke.

"Show me," I commanded, surprising us both with the authority in my tone.

His grin widened, clicking in approval. "Anything my bride desires."

CHAPTER 9

―――――――

YSU

I carried her through the early morning forest, noting how her weight settled against my chest with surprising trust. The little serpent who once trembled at my touch now rested one scarred hand on my shoulder, her fingers tracing the armored segments absentmindedly. My venom had changed something within her. She carried a different scent now, something dangerous mixing with that ancestral green that had first caught my attention.

"You're warmer than before," she observed, her voice carrying none of the careful deference she'd shown mere hours ago.

"Your perception sharpens," I replied, adjusting my grip as we navigated the twisting roots of the forest. "It has been quite some time since I've had such a satisfying meal. Their essence fuels me."

She hummed thoughtfully, a sound that vibrated against my chest. Such a small thing, yet I found myself cataloging it alongside her other responses—the way her breath no longer caught when my additional arms shifted, how her pulse remained steady even when my mandibles clicked near her ear. Fear had transmuted into something far more intriguing.

The villa emerged from the morning mist, rigid and unnatural. Roman stone and precise angles assaulted the natural curves of the hillside, though my silk now decorated its walls in ghostly streams. Bodies hung suspended from windows and doorways, wrapped in white cocoons that shifted gently in the breeze. The heating system still breathed its hot air, though now it carried the copper scent of spilled blood rather than perfumed oils.

"It looks different," she murmured, tilting her head as she studied her former home. "Smaller."

"You are no longer the tiny creature that was once imprisoned here." I set her down at the villa's entrance, watching how she moved. Already I saw change. Her gait was more fluid. She hadn't noticed that her steps made no sound on the stone, or that her balance had shifted to accommodate changes yet to come. She sniffed the air, searching for her quarry. Already my little serpent was becoming something much more deadly.

We passed through halls painted with arterial spray, over floors where drag marks told stories of futile attempts at escape. I would have to reward her for it—I hadn't had such fun in ages. The thought of it stirred the hunger inside me, but I wasn't sure whether it rose for the hunt...or for the way I intended to spread her beneath me and feast again.

She paused at a doorway—her former room, I surmised from the way her jaw tightened. But she didn't enter. She didn't linger. The past held less power when the future promised such exquisite possibilities.

"You said you had a gift for me," she prompted, full of naked desire that had me grinning.

"Such a greedy little thing." I guided her to the triclinium, where torchlight flickered over the scene I'd arranged with particular care. "I thought you might appreciate the chance to conclude certain unfinished business."

The large one hung suspended from the ceiling, silk binding him from shoulder to ankle. His own bulk betrayed him; his weight dragged him downward so his limbs had nearly lost all blood. His face purpled above the wrappings, eyes bulging as he recognized first me, then her. Muffled sounds escaped the gag of webbing across his mouth—threats or prayers to deaf gods. I didn't particularly care.

Beside him, the young one with a hand for artistry presented a more pathetic sight. I'd wrapped him loosely, allowing his arms some movement so he could struggle. The boy's face streamed with tears and snot, his whole body shaking as he watched her approach.

I had smelled her on them. Knew they had been the worst offenders of her harm. The void within me had begged to consume them as I had so many others, but a new sensation— the one she had awakened—had allowed me to maim them only, saving them for their true justice.

How different they must have looked to her now—these men who once seemed powerful as they held her down, who made her so desperate she bargained herself to a creature of nightmare to destroy them. But they were just human. Unlike her. Not anymore.

"They're still alive," she said, and I heard the tremble in her voice.

"Fresh meat spoils quickly," I explained, settling myself against a pillar to observe. "I thought you might prefer them aware."

She stopped before the large one, her face unreadable.

What is my serpent thinking? She traced her hand down along his side, not quite touching. He tried to follow her movement, straining against the silk.

"He liked to kick me here," she rasped, indicating her ribs. "Broke three of them once. Said it was to teach me proper posture."

I clicked my mandibles in acknowledgment but remained silent. This was her moment to seize or squander.

A sword lay on the floor where its owner had dropped it. One of many scattered weapons that had proven useless against me. She bent to retrieve it, testing its weight with an untrained hand. The blade caught the torchlight as she returned to the brute.

"You always said pain was instructive," she told him, voice steady as deep water. I held back my sound of satisfaction. "Let me return the lesson."

The blade entered just below his ribs, angled upward with surprising accuracy. His muffled scream harmonized beautifully with the wet sound of parting flesh. But she didn't stop. She withdrew the blade and struck again, and again. An artery burst and blood sprayed across her rage-filled face.

Devastating.

I longed to wrap her in my arms, to lick all that fresh blood from her soft skin until I sank into her warm cunt, her taste and the taste of her revenge merging. But there would be time for that later.

"This is for every night you held me down. This is for the burns. This is for making me watch while you—" Her voice broke, but her arm didn't waver. Blood soaked through the silk wrappings, spreading like spilled wine across a pristine white cloth.

When the brute finally stilled, she stepped back, breathing hard. The sword dripped on the tiles. Already I saw the shift— her pupils dilated and elongated, her chest rising and falling with excitement rather than exertion.

"How do you feel?" I asked, genuinely curious.

She considered, her head tilting in a gesture unconsciously mirrored from my own mannerisms. *Adorable.*

"Nothing. I thought it would...fill something. Feel better."

"Because you merely killed him. Any peasant with a sharp stick can kill." I moved closer, careful not to touch her yet. "You felt nothing because you gave him nothing of yourself. Death alone doesn't satisfy—consumption does."

Her gaze shifted to the boy, who had worked one arm partially free and clawed frantically at his bonds. The boy's terror filled the air, sharp and intoxicating. He had nearly gotten free, the pathetic thing. She approached him slowly, and I noted with interest how her body crouched low automatically. A predator with prey in its sights.

"Please," he managed to gasp as she reached for his bindings. "Please, I was just following orders, I never wanted—"

"Liar." The word emerged as a hiss. She dropped the sword and tore the webbing with her bare hands—her nails, I noted with satisfaction, had sharpened, and she didn't notice the strength required. She circled him as he scrambled backward on hands and knees, every movement one of a hunter.

"You loved it," she spat. "Loved leaving your little marks, your signatures in my skin. You found others when I no longer satisfied you. You called me moon-whore. Said my barbarian blood made me fit only for bleeding and fucking."

He tried to run. It was almost pitiable how slowly he moved compared to her now. She caught him at the doorway, one hand closing on his shoulder with enough force to pulverize bone. His scream transformed into something higher, more primal, as I heard them crunch.

"No more knives for you," she snarled, and then she was on him.

What followed transcended simple violence. She tore into him with hands that no longer quite qualified as human, fingernails rending flesh like claws. Parts of him came away in her grip, and she flung them aside with disgust before diving back in.

He tried to fight back, landing a solid blow to her jaw that would have felled her yesterday. Today, she barely noticed. She responded by grabbing his striking arm and pulling. The sick, wet pop of separation from socket preceded his shriek by a heartbeat.

"You liked to cut patterns," she panted, using those sharpened nails to peel skin in strips. "Let me show you what I learned."

I watched, fascinated, as she systematically dismantled him. There was artistry in her fury now—she targeted the places that hurt most but killed slowest. When he begged, she forced his mouth open and ripped out his tongue. When he tried to crawl away, she cut his tendons, just as efficient a trap as my web.

The hunger had taken her fully now. Her jaw began to unhinge and her throat elongated as she leaned over his gurgling form. The serpent awakened in truth, drawn by the warm feast spread before it. I saw the moment she wanted to consume him—really consume him, not merely kill—but her body hadn't progressed enough for such ambitions.

Instead, she tore out his throat with her teeth.

When she finally rose, she was painted in crimson from

mouth to waist. Gore dripped from her sharpened nails, and when she smiled, her teeth had elongated into fangs. Her transformation accelerated with each act of savagery, her body rushing to match the predator her spirit already was. Her pupils were blown wide, nearly obscuring the soft honey brown. *Perfection.*

"Better?" I inquired.

She shook her head, and I watched the fangs recede. "I wanted to swallow him whole," she admitted, voice rough with desire she didn't fully understand. "I could feel my throat trying to...change."

"Patience, neidr. Your body learns what your soul already knows." I stepped over the boy's scattered remains, noting with approval how thoroughly she had destroyed him. "The consumption will come when you're ready."

She looked down at her bloodied hands, flexing fingers that now moved just slightly wrong, joints bending at angles human anatomy shouldn't allow. "What's happening to me? What did you do to me?"

I frowned. "You're becoming what you were meant to be," I corrected, unable to resist running a finger along her jaw, feeling the subtle scaling beginning beneath her skin. "My venom can't awaken what doesn't already linger within your heart."

The bloodlust faded, and I saw the human part of her balk as she tried to wipe the blood from her hands. "I'm becoming a monster." Tears welled in her eyes.

I wrapped my hand around her face, forcing her to look at me. "What drew you into the wildwood under the blood moon of Samhain? Be honest, little human."

She didn't squirm in my grip. "You called me. When they

held me down, I heard your voice in my ear, telling me to come find you."

I studied her eyes. With the hunger gone, the golden flecks swimming in the soft brown of her irises shone like the sunlight she would never be comfortable in again. But in them, I saw no lie.

The wind rose, slamming the shutters of this cursed tomb to humanity, and I heard laughter in it I had ignored for centuries.

"It was not I who called you, but that part of you they could not tame. The wildness that revels in darkness and death, the old magic that craves the taste of blood—for blood is always honest."

Her eyes went wide, but I knew she felt the truth in it. Something in her expression shifted—a shadow of disappointment she tried to hide but couldn't quite manage.

"So you didn't call to me? I thought..." Her voice came out smaller than before, and she looked away. "I thought you wanted me to fight back. But I was just another creature stumbling into your domain."

The hurt in her tone caught me off guard. For three centuries, I had been content with solitude, with the endless cycle of hunt and feed the curse demanded. Yet watching her withdraw, seeing that spark of connection dim, stirred something I had thought long dead.

"You think yourself so unimportant?" I asked, forcing my voice to remain steady. "Do you believe coincidence brought you to my grove on the one night when the veil was thinnest? That chance alone made you the first in three hundred years to survive my venom?"

She looked back at me then, searching my face for deception, but I continued before she could speak.

"The forest may have called to the wildness in your blood, but I chose to answer when you called my name. I chose to bargain with you when I could have simply taken what I needed and left the rest for the insects." My thumb brushed her bloodstained cheek. "I chose to keep you."

Her lips parted slightly, hope warring with caution in her expression.

"Men have always fooled themselves," I said, my voice roughening despite my efforts. "With riches, with gold, with their grand villas and conquests. They tell themselves they possess what they desire, that ownership brings satisfaction. But they are wrong about possession, just as you are wrong about your worth."

I leaned closer, close enough that her warm breath ghosted across my cheek.

"Three hundred years of prey have passed through my woods. Desperate souls, broken creatures, those seeking death or power or escape. None of them made me wonder what they might become. None made me curious about tomorrow. None made me realize that perhaps the curse had not taken everything from me after all."

The words escaped before I could stop them, more revelation than I intended. But seeing her eyes widen, watching the way her breath caught, I found I did not regret the admission.

"The magic in you knows that in the end, we all return to the same earth. Even creatures like you and I. But until that end..." I paused, wrestling with concepts I had not entertained for centuries. "Until then, perhaps we need not walk alone."

"You and I..." she echoed softly, the corners of her eyes warming.

She leaned into my touch then—this fierce little thing who had just reduced her tormentor to wet fragments—and warmth stirred in my chest. Pride, perhaps. But deeper still, something far more dangerous.

"What about...him?" She gestured toward the lord's chambers. "You saved him for me as well?"

My grin spread wide enough to show all my teeth. "Oh yes. Are you ready to end this, neidr?"

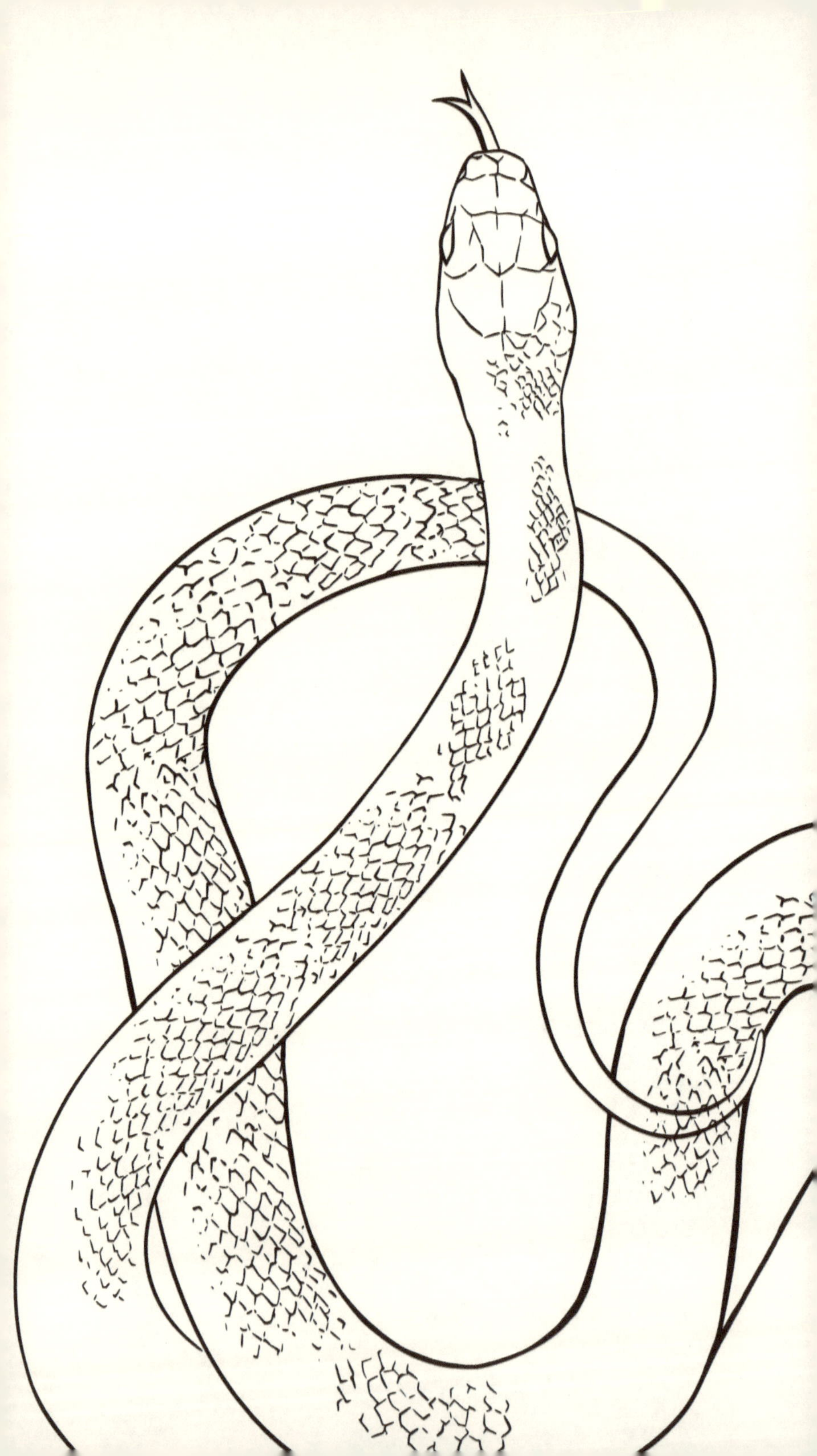

CHAPTER 10

FLAVIA

The corridor to Tiberius' chambers stretched before me, somehow feeling like an insurmountable distance. My bare feet left bloody prints on the pristine tiles— Gaius' blood, Marcus' blood, the blood of what I was becoming. Behind me, Ysu moved with patient silence, tracking my every movement with an interest that felt heavy.

I had destroyed them. I had killed Marcus and torn Gaius to pieces—and I had enjoyed it. Ysu had said it was not his venom, but what I had always been, only awakened. Had I always been a monster, or was that a lie meant to stop me from fighting this transformation? Did I want to fight it?

The great oak doors were shattered, a few shards of wood still clinging to the hinges, blocking my view into the room. But I could smell him—fear-sweat and that particular cologne he imported from Rome at ruinous expense. My senses were heightened; I could feel that now. Even without sight, I felt the despair that permeated the air, and my tongue flicked out, trying to taste it.

I pushed past the wreckage, revealing the man who had orchestrated years of my torment.

Tiberius was strung up in a fashion reminiscent of the crucifixions the Romans loved so much. His arms were outstretched, his head hung against his chest. His toga was torn, held in place by the silver threads of Ysu's web, and dark hair streaked with gray hid his face. But when we entered, his head shot up, his eyes finding mine, and something shifted in his expression. The terror remained, but beneath it bloomed terrible recognition.

"Flavia." My name on his lips sounded like an accusation. "My Flavia, what have you done?"

I stepped into the room, aware of how I must look—my clothing torn and barely covering me, my feet and nails dirty and streaked with blood. Every bit the barbarian he believed me to be. The hunger coiled in my belly, urging me forward. It matched the tingling that simmered beneath my skin constantly now. This was the moment I had dreamed of through countless nights of agony.

"Look at you," he continued, and his voice carried genuine sorrow. "I tried so hard to keep you pure. To stop the sickness in your veins. Your father begged me, you know. He said it was your mother's dying wish, to protect you from what you might become."

I froze. What in the hells was he talking about?

"You're lying."

He laughed, bitter and broken. "She knew what ran in your blood. The curse of her line. She tasked your father with protecting you, but he was weak. He made me promise to keep you from the old ways, to beat the wildness out of you before it could take root." His eyes glistened with that cruelty I knew all too well. "Every hurt, every humiliation—it was to save you from this. From becoming the very monster they feared."

My nails dug into my palms, my belly writhed, and my skin tingled as though a thousand insects crawled over me—my entire body reacting to the shame that flared alive inside me.

"Lies! You enjoyed hurting me. You enjoyed having your men hurt me!" The words were ash in my mouth.

"I wanted to save you, my Flavia. You know how precious you were to me."

"Enough." The word tore from my throat with more venom than Ysu had given me. The serpent within me coiled, ready to strike. But another part of me—that horrible, human part—crumbled. The hunger fled, leaving only a gaping emptiness that threatened to swallow me whole.

I turned away, unable to look at him, unable to process the possibility that my mother might have sanctioned my suffering. That maybe her stories weren't warnings about men, but about my own blood.

I stormed toward the door.

"Let him rot here. Let him die slowly, alone with his lies," I muttered, not meeting Ysu's gaze.

I felt Ysu's disappointment—a subtle shift in the air, a pause in his breathing. But he said nothing as I fled the chamber, leaving Tiberius to his entangled fate.

———

The grove felt smaller when we returned. I perched on a fallen log, knees drawn to my chest, while Ysu tended to his web meticulously. He'd been silent during our journey back, offering neither comfort nor condemnation. Now he worked above me, adjusting tensions and reweaving sections with a focus that seemed deliberately distant.

"You are disappointed in me." The words slipped out before I could stop them.

His movements paused. Eight eyes turned toward me, and in their depths I caught something unexpected—not anger, but a weariness belonging to a creature burdened by centuries.

"Disappointment implies expectation," he said at last, descending with that unnatural grace. "I expected you to kill him. You chose mercy. The fault lies in my assumption, not your decision."

"It wasn't mercy. He'll still suffer as he starves to death." I hugged my knees tighter. "I just...what if he was telling the truth? What if my mother really did—"

"Does it matter?" Ysu settled beside me, two of his spider-like arms bracketing my body. "Whatever the reason for his actions, the result remains. You suffered. You survived. You transformed."

"But if she wanted to protect me from this curse—"

"Humans lie, neidr. To others, to themselves. They wrap their cruelties in false purpose and call it kindness." One clawed finger tilted my chin up. "Your mother may have feared your nature. Or your former husband may have crafted a fiction to wound you one final time. Either way, you are what you are now."

I searched his face. Even with all his additional eyes and strange markings, he felt more human to me than any man I had ever known. "You were cursed?" The stories never said where he came from—only his hunger, his cruelty. But as I felt changes in my body mimicking his, I couldn't help wondering.

His eight eyes blinked, out of sync. "Yes. Long ago."

"So you were human once? Do you ever wonder who you would have been, if the curse hadn't changed you?"

Something flickered across his expression—vulnerability quickly shuttered. "I was a warlord who chose pride over my people's survival. I craved power and consumption, and I took what I thought I deserved. The curse merely revealed what was already there."

His mandibles clicked softly. "Had I stayed a man, my fate was sealed. I would not have changed, and my greed would have consumed me, just as it does now."

"But the curse—it changed you?"

Was he frozen by this ancient magic, locked into what he was? Would it curse me in the same way, consumed forever by my rage? Or was there something more waiting for us?

His gaze held me as a gentle claw stroked my cheek. "I'm beginning to believe it has, in ways I did not expect. I never thought loneliness would be the greatest burden of them all."

The admission hung between us, a fragile thing I wanted to cradle. I reached out and traced the edge where flesh met chitin along his jaw. "You're not alone now."

"No," he agreed, catching my hand. "Though you may yet make me wish I were."

Despite the weight in my stomach, I smiled. "Because I denied you your grand finale?"

"Because you complicate things." His grip tightened—not painfully, but with emphasis. "I haven't had to consider another's feelings and needs in centuries. It's...inconvenient."

"Poor ancient creature," I murmured. "Brought low by one broken human girl."

"Hardly human anymore." One of his arms slid around my waist, lifting me against him. "You are strong. I've seen grown men shit themselves at the mere sight of me. I've heard them scream from pain minuscule compared to what you endured. They cowered and begged for their lives, shaking like newborn fawns. But not you. You did not flinch or cower. You bargained." His mandibles clicked with something like pride.

"You had nothing, and still within moments you had me twisted around your little finger. You have endured, my neidr. Most would not survive what you have. But you did. And now I will have the pleasure of watching that pain transform into something much darker. So no—you are far from broken. Bent, perhaps. Then reforged."

"Like a blade?"

"Like a chain."

Heat rippled through me, the serpent stirring with interest. "Is that what you want? To bind me?"

His multiple eyes darkened. "Would you let me?"

The question hung heavy with promise. I thought of Tiberius' chains, of years spent bound and helpless. But this— this was different. This was choice.

"Show me," I whispered.

Ysu's smile revealed too many teeth. "Dangerous words, neidr."

Shadows curled around him as he shifted into his more human form, though he still held me between his spider-like arms.

He stood, lifting me with effortless strength. He guided my hands behind my back, forearms pressed together. His human hands wove silk around my wrists—not the harsh binding of his web, but something softer.

"The difference," he said, pulling the silk just tight enough to feel restrictive, "is your willingness. You can break these easily. They hold only because you allow it."

The silk was cool against my skin. He worked with an

artist's care, hands tracing up my arms, looping and looping, the pressure triggering that incessant tingling under my skin.

The position was uncomfortable, but not painful. My chest was thrust forward, exposed to him as he tugged the few remaining shreds of my clothing away. His hands wandered the scarred expanses of my skin, and the tingling grew until I ached. My breasts felt heavier, weighted by craving and desire.

His hand slid around my ribs as his thumb toyed with one overly sensitive nipple. "Do you trust me?" he asked, his main eyes locked on my chest but his others watching my expression warily.

A dangerous question. Pain had become the only constant in my life. In some ways, I knew it better than anything else, and in that, there was familiarity. I knew how to lose myself in it, how to harden myself. But what he was asking would open me to a different kind of pain—one I had no resistance to. A venom for which I had no immunity.

"I trust you."

His eyebrow rose. "Some would deem it unwise to trust a monster like me."

"You did tell me I was likely very stupid."

His grin split wide, and he leaned forward, his long tongue dragging up the length of my neck and along my jaw. "Then let me show you the beauty in surrender."

His tongue snaked into my mouth, its immense length overwhelming me as our lips met. It claimed every surface before he pulled away, his hands never pausing.

He wrapped more silk around my thighs, the pale flesh there bulging against the tight confines. He wove firm knots around my chest, the silk forming a cage for my breasts, trapping the blood in them until the ache was almost unbearable.

My nipples flushed dark, and I squirmed, desperate for his touch.

"Patience," he murmured. "I'll give you everything you need. But only when you're at the edge of what you can handle."

His hands continued their work, the knots tightening little by little. Then he lifted me into the air, leaving me dangling before him like a perverse ornament. My chest strained forward under my own weight, and he bound my calves to my thighs, my legs spread.

But then the panic set in. I was trapped—I was a prisoner. My heart raced, blood rushing to my head, and I struggled. I felt a strand of silk snap before his hands closed around my face.

"My neidr." He was in front of me, all eight eyes fixed on mine. "You are mine. You are safe. No harm will come to you."

My heart slowed, but I still fought the restraints, tears rising in my eyes. "It hurts."

"If it's too much, we will stop."

I stopped struggling and simply watched him. Ever since he had bitten me, all my senses had sharpened. I could feel his heartbeat, steady in his chest. I could smell his cloyingly sweet scent. I'd said I would trust him, but part of me had assumed he wouldn't listen. I could see the hunger in his eyes, sense the way his body had begun to heat with arousal. And still—he stopped.

"You would stop for me? I thought you fed on fear."

His grin vanished, his mouth hardening into a firm line. "I do. But you are no longer my prey. You are mine. Your fear is delicious, but when you embrace it and let it transform into something more, that is what I crave."

Shame rose unbidden, heat blooming across my cheeks and down my neck. "I'm afraid of the pain."

"Does it hurt, or is that your mind playing tricks? Tell me what you really feel."

I was confined—that much I knew. But with his cool hands on my face, I was able to slow my racing heart, and for the first time in memory I let myself focus on what my body was feeling.

The silk was tight, but nothing cut into me. A deep throbbing where blood pooled, an ache where my weight pressed against the restraints. But it wasn't the pain I knew. It didn't speak of cruelty but of possibility.

"I feel...aching. I need you to touch me, Ysu."

He grinned, and I watched as his spider arms tugged on the threads of his web. I was lifted higher, my breasts now level with his mouth. His tongue lashed out, wrapping around one, squeezing it even tighter before he flicked the tip over my aching nipple and I cried out.

My thighs tried to squeeze together, but they were bound apart. Heat flooded my face as arousal slipped down my leg while he continued to lave my nipple with his tongue, his clawed fingers rolling the other between them. Each tug sent my stomach twisting, tears rising in my eyes. Too much blood rushed to my head, everything foggy—he was giving me too much and not enough all at once.

"Ysu..." I choked out, unsure of what I was even asking. Drool dripped from my swollen, tingling lips as I tried to decide whether I wanted him to stop this torture—or never end it.

His tongue extended, licking the droplet from my chin as his spider arms tugged at the silk that held me aloft. The suspension was a mastery of attachments and pulleys, and I flipped over, my back no longer arched. He stepped between my legs, spreading them wider. He traced the length of his lower cock through my soaked heat, and I watched my arousal coat him, slow and glistening.

He tugged another thread, and I rose until I was nearly in a seated position.

"You are mine. I think it's time you take me completely." He grinned.

"You mean...both? At once?" The thought sent shivers through me, and not from fear.

His claws danced over my skin, the tingling becoming almost unbearable. They traced around my swollen breast until I was writhing again. He stroked down both of his cocks, coating his fingers and palm in the thick precum he produced.

Then he swiped his thumb over my clit, circling it torturously slow. With the restraints, the pressure across my body, and the incessant teasing of his claws, I felt ready to combust from that single touch.

His smirk told me he knew it. "We have all night. Why rush?"

"Ysu, if you tease me much more, you may not survive the night." The boldness of my words startled me—almost as much as the heat that rose in his eyes.

"Such a violent thing when angered." His approval dripped from every syllable. His thumb circled tighter, and my legs shook in their restraints. He watched my chest rise and fall with each pant as I got close...so close...

As the pressure in my core built to the point of no return, I felt his other slicked fingers press against the tight ring of my ass.

"Ysu..." I felt myself clench down again.

"You are safe. Surrender to me. Trust me."

He pinched the flesh around my clit, and I drew one last deep breath, forcing myself to relax as my orgasm consumed me.

He groaned in approval, his finger working me open with every shudder of pleasure. He coated himself with more precum before pressing back in with two fingers, slower this time, and the sting was even less.

"If I flip you over, it will be easier—"

"No."

He paused.

"I want to see you." The words admitted more than I wanted, but trust was a sword that cut both ways.

His face revealed nothing, but then his spider arms tugged at the web again so we were face-to-face, and his lips found mine.

It was a tender kiss, not filled with claiming but with something softer. I closed my eyes, swiping my tongue over his bottom lip. He returned the gesture playfully, and something in my chest cracked open. This was what intimacy could be— not just pleasure, but connection.

He continued to toy with me gently, opening me further with his fingers, but he didn't rush. He kissed me, and I knew he would keep kissing me until I was ready. I reveled in the taste of him, the strange sensation of running my tongue over the venom sacs behind his fangs, and the way he shuddered as I did. Small drops of venom emerged, sweet on my tongue. They fed the tingling in my skin until heat built in me again, impossible to ignore.

I pulled back, and all his eyes watched me closely.

"I'm ready."

There was no smirk this time, only reverence as he gathered me in all his arms, positioning himself against me. His fingers withdrew and were replaced with the broad head of his larger cock. He pressed slowly, and the stretch was intense as he entered my cunt and my ass, but he held me close, our breath mingling as he guided my breathing.

"Ysu..."

"I have you, my neidr."

Inch by inch, I took him. It was slow, but inevitable. The tingling of his venom beneath my skin quieted, and all I felt was him.

He bottomed out, and for one more moment he held me close, placing a gentle kiss on my temple. "You're doing so well."

His hand locked around my throat, just tight enough for me to feel my heartbeat beneath his fingers. The other gripped my breast, while his spider limbs held my hips and spread my legs. He slid back before snapping his hips forward, and my eyes rolled back.

Over and over he claimed me, each thrust more desperate than the last. All eight of his eyes squeezed shut as his grip tightened, and I realized he was just as overcome as I was.

"Ysu, look at me."

His gaze locked with mine, and I wanted to touch him more than anything. I struggled to free my arms, and he sliced the silk away with one swift motion. I grabbed his face, pressing his forehead to mine. His dark eyes shimmered in the moonlight, and for a moment there was absolutely no barrier between us.

I kissed him again, and our bodies convulsed in unison, rapture flowing through us as our orgasms chased each other.

"My perfect neidr. In all the dark corners of this world, in all the forgotten places where old magic sleeps, there is nothing more beautiful than you, here in my arms."

CHAPTER 11

YSU

My serpent sat at the heart of my grove, her small hands holding the meal I had brought her. I found myself watching her more and more. Admiring the beautiful curve of her spine, the way her full lips were stained red with fresh blood. In all my long years, she was the most beautiful thing I had ever seen. Like the moonflowers that grew around my spring: pale and fragile in appearance, yet deadly to those who disrespected her power.

But she wasn't eating. She only fidgeted with the meat I had brought her. That wouldn't do at all.

"You need to learn to hunt properly," I said. "This human habit of scavenging from my kills won't sustain you much longer."

She looked up from where she sat cross-legged on the grove floor, the flecks of gold in her eyes catching the moon's light. "I eat what you provide. Isn't that enough?"

"No." I moved closer, brushing hair from her bloodied face. "Your body is changing. It requires fresh blood, fresh meat. The hunt itself feeds your transformation as much as the consumption."

She set aside the half-eaten flesh and wrapped her arms around her knees. "I've killed. Marcus. Gaius. Isn't that hunting?"

"That was revenge. Beautiful, but personal." I paused, searching for words she might understand to explain what had become instinct centuries ago. "Hunting is accepting what you are. Predator. Part of the natural order—not above it, not outside it."

She hid her face, something she rarely did now. "I was human a week ago."

I settled on the ground across from her, close enough to see the faint scaling beginning along her arms. "Were you? Or were you always this, waiting for permission to emerge?"

She was quiet for a long moment. When she spoke, her voice carried a tremor I hadn't heard since our first nights together. "If I hunt—truly hunt—what's left of me? The girl who sang songs in her head during the worst of it, the songs of my ancestors—my people?"

"She remains. But she becomes more." I wanted to reach for her then, realizing it was to comfort, not to consume. Instead, I held still. "You think predators cannot appreciate beauty? Cannot create? I've walked this forest for three centuries, neidr. I know every tree, every stone, every small life that moves through my territory. The hunt doesn't diminish appreciation—it sharpens it."

She lifted her head, studying me with those warm eyes. "Show me, then. But if I ask to stop—"

"We stop." The promise came easily. After what we'd shared, after the trust she'd shown in letting me bind her in silk, I would not break faith over this.

When had I become so soft-hearted?

————

The forest breathed differently at night when one moved as a hunter. I watched my serpent follow me through the under-brush, noting how her movements had already begun to adapt. Not the flowing grace she would eventually achieve, but better than the clumsy creature who'd first stumbled into my grove.

"There," I whispered, pointing to tracks in the soft earth. "Deer. Young buck, from the depth of the print. Perhaps an hour ahead."

She crouched beside the marks, and I caught myself admiring the curve of her spine, the way moonlight caught in her hair. Dangerous thoughts—not of possession this time, but of something softer. More and more frequently, I found myself craving not just her body but her presence. The way she challenged me. The way she trusted me despite everything I was.

"How do you know it's male?" she asked, pulling me from my reverie.

"The drag marks here. Young bucks testing their antlers against bark." I moved behind her, close enough to feel her warmth. "Close your eyes. What else can you sense?"

She obeyed, nostrils flaring slightly, her tongue flicking out. "I smell...musk? And something fresh."

"He's been feeding on the young shoots near the stream. Follow that scent."

We tracked in silence for nearly an hour. I stayed behind her, letting her find the trail, correcting only when she veered too far off course. Part of me wanted to simply show her, to demonstrate my centuries of skill. But watching her learn, watching her mind work through each puzzle, had become its own pleasure.

When we finally spotted the buck drinking at a moonlit pool, she froze.

"I can't," she breathed. "It's...beautiful."

The deer was beautiful. Young and strong, its coat catching silver light as it lifted its head to scan for danger. I understood her hesitation. But I also understood what she needed to become to survive in a world full of humans who wanted nothing more than to crush what they did not understand.

"Beauty and death aren't opposites," I said softly. "Watch."

I moved swiftly, circling wide to approach from down-wind. The buck never sensed me until my hand was already at its neck. One quick motion, and it dropped without suffering —life to death in a heartbeat.

My serpent approached slowly, her face unreadable. "You didn't make it suffer. I thought you fed on fear?"

I chuckled. "I do, but human fear. Humans have tried to remove themselves from the natural order. When they are faced with the realization that they are not as powerful as they've deluded themselves into believing, nothing is sweeter. But the creatures of this forest? They understand the order of things. Their suffering serves no purpose."

She kneeled beside the deer, running her hand along its flank. "Tiberius made everything suffer. Said it made the meat sweeter."

"Tiberius was a fool." The words came out harsher than intended. Even trapped in my web, his shadow lingered over too many of our conversations.

I often regretted letting him live. Seeing her now, how anything could have wanted to harm her, set anger simmering in my core unlike anything I had felt before. My own foolish indifference to her when we first met haunted me almost as much as the ghost of her former husband. The marks on her skin I had once merely observed now filled me with visions of his blood and organs smeared across tiled floors after I'd made him scream for hours.

But it was not my place. I knew when the time was right, my serpent would find the strength she needed, and it would be glorious. Still, I wished I could free her from the mental cage of his making. "Cruelty is not strength. You survived him because you were stronger, not crueler."

She looked up at me, and in the moonlight I could see tears threatening. "Sometimes I think I survived because I was too cowardly to die."

The hollow sensation in my chest intensified. Without thinking, I pulled her against me, her back to my chest, arms wrapped around her. I found myself wishing I could pull all her worry and pain into myself, so I could bear that burden for her. A dangerous feeling indeed.

"You survived because you had fire within you he could never extinguish," I said against her hair. "Every time he tried to diminish you, you endured. That's not cowardice. That's the kind of strength that remakes worlds."

She relaxed into my hold, and we stayed like that. I found myself not wanting to move, not wanting to return to the grove where old patterns drove me to coldness. Here, holding her, I could admit what I'd been denying since she had awakened in my web.

I was falling into something I had no name for. She filled my every waking thought. Her warmth and her challenges had become part of my daily existence, shifting from possibility to necessity. I had trapped her in my web, but now I was the one whose heart was ensnared.

"Tomorrow," she said finally, "I'll try to hunt. Properly."

"Tomorrow," I agreed, still not releasing her.

But inside, the hunter who'd walked alone for centuries wondered what he would do when she no longer needed these lessons—when she became the predator she was meant to be. Would she still choose to remain?

I would allow nothing else. After a lifetime of endless hunger, I did not think that I was greedy enough to still crave more. But I did. I craved her in a way that dwarfed the ancient magic of my curse. What was hunger when she gave me everything I needed? No matter the cost, I would keep her with me until the very earth cracked away beneath our feet.

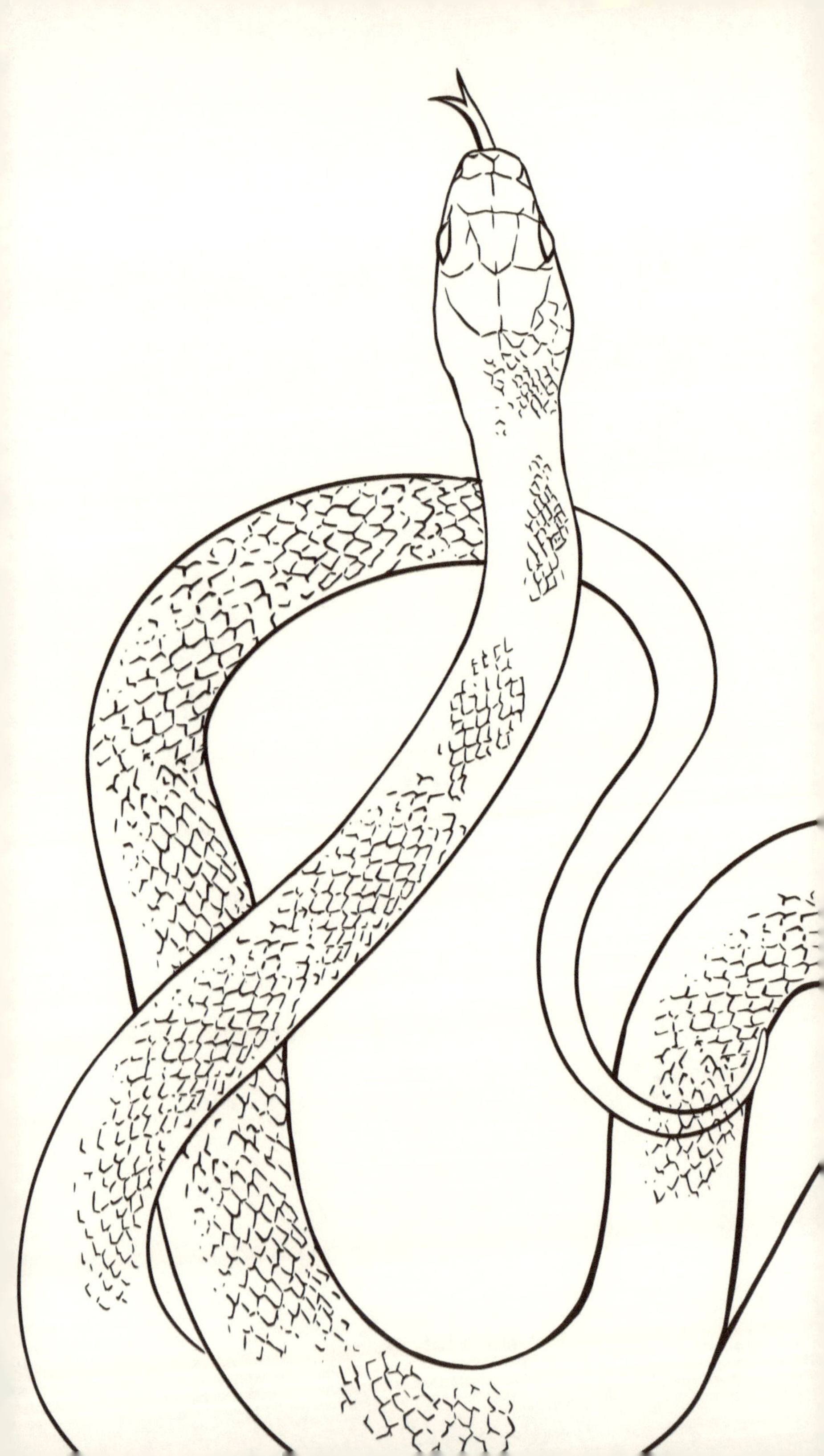

Chapter 12

Flavia

The forest dreamed through me—or perhaps I dreamed through it—the boundaries dissolving like mist between ancient trees.

I moved through undergrowth that parted around me, my body flowing in serpentine patterns that felt more natural than walking ever had. It felt right, just as Ysu had said. A part of me that had only been waiting to awaken.

The Roman scout ahead crashed through bracken with the graceless noise of civilization, his bronze armor catching the moonlight in flashes that announced his position to every predator within miles.

My tongue flicked out, tasting his fear-sweat on the air. He was young, barely past his first campaign season, sent to patrol borders his commanders no longer truly controlled. The leather of his sandals was still stiff and fresh from the armory.

Foolish humans, a voice that sounded like Ysu whispered through my consciousness, though I knew he slept back in the grove. *They send children to map territory that was never theirs to claim.*

But as I descended from the canopy, the voice shifted, deepened—becoming something older than even Ysu. The trees themselves spoke, their roots pulsing with words that tasted of mycelium and blood and patient fury.

The roads cut us. The stones suffocate our soil. Their ordered grids carve wounds that will not heal.

The scout stopped to drink from his waterskin, oblivious to how the shadows had changed around him. I could see the pulse in his throat, count the rapid heartbeats that revealed exhaustion and unease. He was lost—had been for hours—though he didn't yet realize the forest had been guiding him in circles, eating up his markers and shifting his path.

Show them what they cannot tame, the forest commanded, and my jaw began to ache with transformation.

I dropped silently behind him, my body elongating in ways that no longer frightened me. He turned at the last moment, eyes widening as he took in what I'd become—neither woman nor serpent but something between, something impossible.

His scream died in his throat as mine opened wider than any human mouth should. The forest held him still, roots tangling his feet, branches ensuring he could not flee. I tasted his terror as my transformed jaw accepted what it was meant for, swallowing him in sections that should have horrified me but only satisfied the deep hunger.

Yes, the ancient voice thrummed through soil and stone. *Let them know their empire will end, but we will always endure. For every tree they fell, every road they build, a new monster will be born.*

I felt the scout's life force spreading through me, not merely sustaining my body but feeding something larger. The forest drank through me, using me as a conduit for its patient rage. I knew that each Roman life I claimed returned strength to the wounded land.

The scene wavered. My consciousness tried to return to my sleeping body, but the forest wouldn't let me go—not yet.

More will come, the voice promised. *They always send more. And you will be waiting, my serpent. You and others like you. What they thought conquered will devour them from within.*

Ysu wrapped several arms around my body, his physical presence pulling me out of the dream. His touch was protective. Possessive. He was satisfied with my hunger, but beneath that, I felt a hesitation.

I was no longer just Flavia seeking revenge. I was the forest's rage given form, its answer to centuries of systematic destruction. And somewhere in the ordered villas and geometric cities, Romans slept uneasily, dreaming of roots cracking through their foundations and shadows with too many teeth.

The dream claimed me again, and I saw them—others like me. Old blood singing with ancient magic, humanity and nature merging into new demons who stalked the night.

I woke with dirt beneath my nails and the taste of bronze on my tongue, wrapped in Ysu's silk while he watched me with all eight eyes.

"It has been many nights since you've had a nightmare, my neidr." He traced a cool hand down my cheek. "What disturbs you?"

I swallowed again; I could still taste that soldier on my tongue. It had just been a dream, hadn't it? The wind picked up, and I swore I heard laughing. Ysu's grip tightened around me.

"It wasn't a nightmare."

Had I changed so much that the thought of swallowing a

man whole no longer disturbed me? That I found the embrace of a monster all I needed?

I curled tight to Ysu's chest, and he relaxed as I traced the dark markings that whorled over his skin.

"Sleep now, my spider." I wove my fingers through his hair, and he emitted a sound almost like purring until his chest rose and fell in the soft rhythm of sleep.

But as I drifted, the wind rose again, its laughter tracing a cold finger down my spine.

CHAPTER 13

FLAVIA

The grove had changed since I had first arrived. Ysu's web had grown, silver strands threading through the forest. My sleeping hammock hung low, and he had built new webs around it, more intricate than anywhere else. A beautiful canopy of his art, the threads forming tessellations and patterns I hadn't seen before. Had he done this purposefully, to surround me with beauty? A part of me suspected he hadn't even realized what he was doing, and the thought brought a smile to my face. *My soft-hearted monster.*

I stood beneath it, bare feet pressed into moss, watching as the moonlight caught in the water droplets like tiny stars. Delicate blue flowers caressed my ankles in the night breeze, and I felt richer than any centurion in their dead homes of stone. Here, everything belonged to the same beautiful cycle, and even if it meant sharing my sleep with creatures of every sort, I knew this was home.

Something snagged in the web; the whole structure jostled, and tiny beads of dew fell across my face, a cool kiss. I wondered what prey Ysu's web had snared—then I heard it.

The forest's call. It spoke exactly as it had in my dream, except this time, it was no dream.

Come deeper, it whispered. *The invaders build a new outpost to the north. They think stone walls will protect them from what stalks the wilds.*

My body swayed toward the summons, muscles tightening with the instinct to change into something swift and silent. Hunger rose in me—not mine alone, but the land's appetite flowing through me like sap.

"Going somewhere, neidr?"

Ysu's voice came from directly behind me, though I hadn't heard him approach. For all his size, he was still a hunter and annoyingly quiet when he wished. I turned to find him in his full form, mandibles slightly spread, every eye fixed on me with an intensity that made my skin prickle.

"The forest calls," I said. "There's prey to the north."

"The forest." Something sharp lay beneath his calm tone. "Yes, it speaks to you often now, doesn't it? Whispers in your dreams, fills your mind with its ancient purposes."

Something in his posture—the way his chitinous limbs held perfectly still while his human hands flexed—sent a warning through me that had nothing to do with my enhanced senses.

"You knew this would happen. You've heard its call." It wasn't a question so much as an accusation.

He crossed his arms over his chest, a very human gesture of petulance that almost made me laugh. "Yes, it calls to all of us. It thinks itself terribly righteous. This curse binds me to it, but I have learned to ignore it."

"You said I was becoming something more. I must go to it."

He hissed. "I said you were changing, but you are mine."

The words emerged with a chittering underlayer that betrayed his agitation. He moved closer, his massive form casting shadows even in the darkness. "Mine to teach. Mine to keep. *Mine.*"

"But I'm also—"

"Nothing else." His hands seized my shoulders while his spider limbs wove around me, not quite restraining but certainly containing. "You are nothing else. The forest may have called you here, but I claimed you. My venom runs through your veins. My web shelters your sleep."

The possessiveness should have reminded me of Tiberius, of ownership enforced through violence. Instead, heat curled through me—dark recognition of a predator who would tear the world apart rather than share his prize.

"The forest—"

"The forest can find another fool to wield as its weapon," he snapped, mandibles clicking inches from my face. "It has waited centuries—it can wait longer. You belong in my web, where I can see you, touch you, ensure no ancient power thinks to steal you."

I tested his grip and found it unyielding, but beneath that immense strength I felt something else.

"You're afraid."

The accusation hung between us. His multiple eyes blinked in sequence—surprise, anger, and vulnerability flashing through them before he found his cold mask again.

"I fear nothing," he replied, though his hands gentled on my shoulders. "I am simply...protective."

"I thought only humans lied, Ysu." I leaned into his hold rather than fighting it. "You're afraid I'll choose the forest over you. That I'll disappear into the deep woods and become something beyond your reach."

His silence spoke volumes. When he finally responded, his voice carried centuries of solitude. "Everything I have ever claimed has been taken by time or hunger or the simple nature of mortal things. You are...different. Changing. Becoming something that might endure as I endure." His hands cupped my face. "I would not lose you to the very power I helped awaken."

"Then come with me," I said. "Hunt with me. Let the forest see what you've made me."

"No." The word cracked like breaking stone. "You hunt in my territory, where my web can track your movements. Where I can follow the vibrations of your victories and feast on your conquests when you return." His grip tightened. "The deep forest has its own guardians, its own hungers. I will not risk you to them."

"You can't cage me, Ysu." Even as I said it, my body reacted to his proximity, to the tenderness blooming beneath all his menace, however he tried to disguise it. The serpent in my belly coiled with different appetites. "A silk prison is still a prison."

His smile revealed all his teeth. "You forget, neidr—you gave yourself to me completely. Mind, body, and soul, sworn beneath the blood moon. The forest may call, but you answer to me first."

He lifted me effortlessly over his shoulder, carrying me back toward the heart of his domain despite my half-hearted struggles. His hand traced up the back of my thigh before gripping the flesh of my ass until his nails bit in, and all thoughts of leaving fled my mind. The forest's whispers faded with each step, replaced by the singing of his web as it recognized its mistress returning.

"This discussion is not over," I warned as he set me down

in our usual resting place, silk already beginning to wind around my ankles.

"No," he agreed, but his wide smile told me the truth. He settled his massive form around me like a living cage. "But you are mine, neidr. The forest will have to make do with lesser servants. I did not wait three centuries to share you with anything—not Romans, not gods, and certainly not the ambitious dreams of trees."

His possessiveness wrapped around me tighter than any web, and I found myself torn between the wild calling of the hunt and the dark comfort of being so thoroughly ensnared. In the distance, I could feel the forest's patience, vast and implacable.

It would wait. But Ysu's eyes promised he would not.

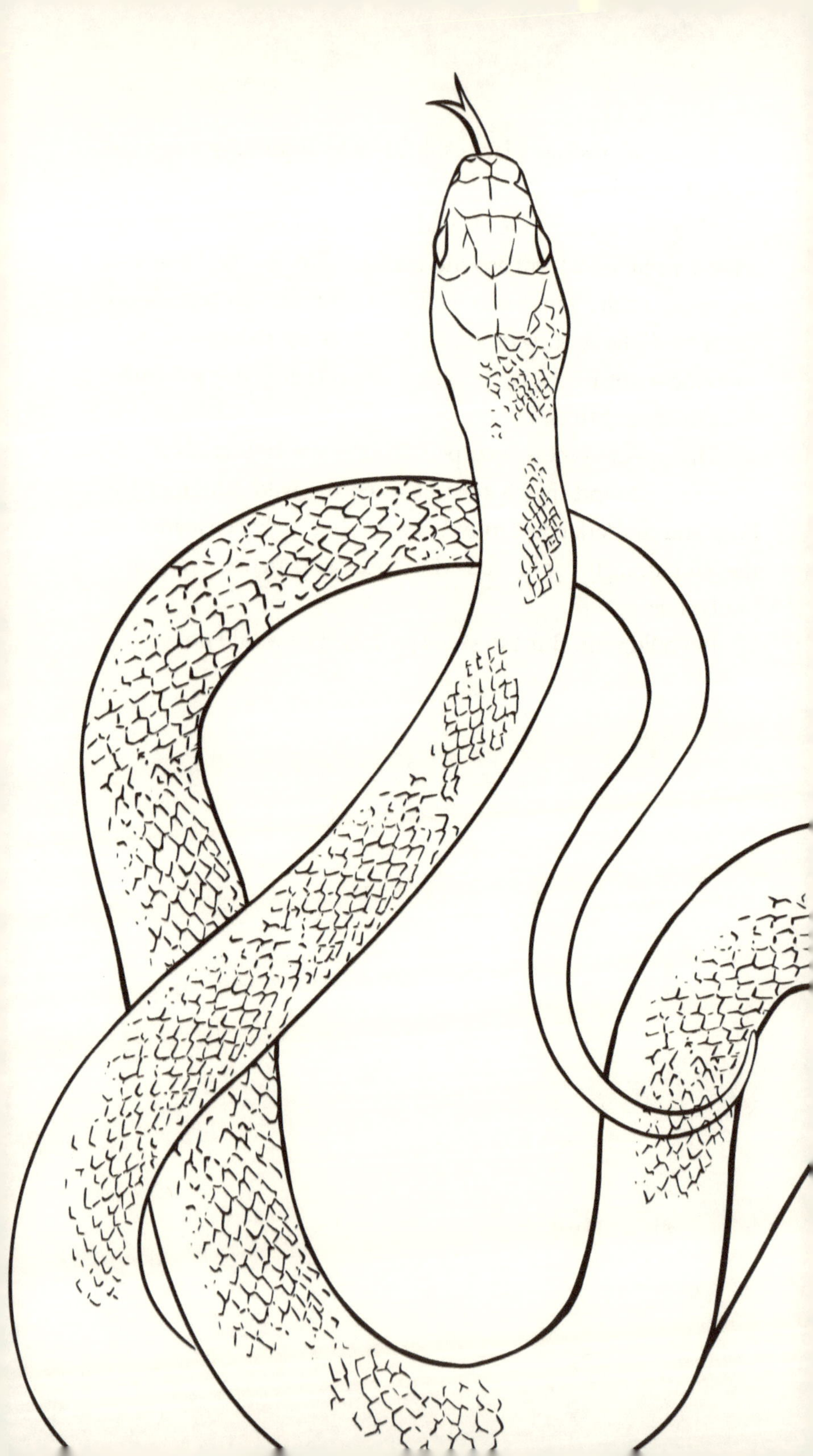

Chapter 14

Flavia

Sleep never found me. I listened to the steady sound of Ysu's breathing as night crept toward day, but my mind never stilled. I kept hearing the whispers of the forest in every fluttering leaf, in every drop of morning dew.

Come to me. Come to me and devour them all.

Ysu had wrapped me in his silk, but he had been right before. I broke out of the restraints easily, my body now far stronger than any human's. I moved across his web like it was my own domain, not causing a single vibration. Perhaps he had taught me too well.

I dropped to the forest floor without a sound and looked up to see him still curled, sleeping soundly.

I would return—there was never any doubt of that in my mind. Ysu was mine as much as I was his. But I needed to see what I could be on my own.

I wandered deeper into the wildwood, not following any path or game trail, guided purely by instinct. The wind pulled me forward, and I swore I could feel the forest's delight with each step I took closer to its heart.

The trees closed in around me, and I was reminded of the first night I had entered these woods. But I was not her anymore. Now, I was something that belonged here.

But I was still being hunted. I sensed the movement overhead, attuned now to the vibration in the forest. I wondered if he would ever be able to sneak up on me again.

I dashed forward, hearing branches crack above as he followed. I was fast now, but he was still faster. His shadow descended, and we tumbled to the ground, his weight pressing me into the soft earth.

"Going somewhere without permission?" His voice carried no sleep, no surprise. He'd been awake—watching, waiting.

I twisted in his grip, testing my new strength against his. "The forest calls. I told you—"

"The forest." He flipped me onto my back, pinning my wrists above my head with his human hands while his spider limbs caged me against the ground. "Always the forest. Tell me, does it whisper sweetly to you? Does it promise power and freedom?" His face lowered until his breath brushed my cheek. "Does it make you forget who gave you the revenge you craved so deeply?"

"I haven't forgotten anything."

One clawed finger traced the spot on my neck where he had first pumped me full of his venom. "You've forgotten that you swore yourself to me. Or were those just pretty words to get what you wanted?"

I met his eight eyes steadily. "I need to know what I can do alone."

"Alone." The word dripped venom. "There is no alone for you anymore. I am in your blood." His grip tightened. "Do you think I spent centuries in solitude just to watch you wander off the moment you grow strong enough to break my silk?"

"You can't keep me trapped forever."

His mouth stretched into that too-wide smile. "You should have thought of that before I carved our names into the roots of this world. Before I pulled the threads of fate and wove them into a web from which you could never escape."

That smile broke across his face as his dark hair brushed my cheek.

"But if you want to run, by all means, run. It's been so long since I've had a satisfying hunt. But know this—when I catch you, I may not feel as merciful as I do now. I want to see just how far I can push this new, strong body of yours."

My heart raced with anticipation. I wanted that too.

The prey I'd caught in the woods wasn't an adversary. It wasn't a creature of nightmare and shadow I could unleash myself on without fear of permanent harm.

He was.

I would wind myself around him, squeeze him until he couldn't stand it, and have him fill me completely.

I traced my hands up his broad form, across the dark whorled marks that climbed his neck, until my nails raked over his scalp. I dragged them into his flesh until all eight of his eyes rolled back in pleasure.

"Then catch me if you can."

I tucked my knees to my chest and slammed my feet into his torso. In a testament to my new strength, he flew back, crashing into a tree as I scrambled to my feet.

I ran.

My heartbeat thundered in my ears, but it was a steady rhythm now, not the frantic hammering of prey. My eyes shifted, the darkness peeling away like shed skin. Every root, every stone, every low-hanging branch revealed itself in sharp relief. My bare feet found purchase on moss-slick rock, my body moving around obstacles with ease.

Behind me, I heard nothing—which meant he was already hunting. The silence of it sent thrills down my spine that had nothing to do with fear.

Everything to do with anticipation.

His venom—and the creature I was becoming—sang through my veins with each stride. My muscles lengthened, strengthened, propelling me through the undergrowth faster than any human could move. I tasted the air with a tongue that was now split, tracking his scent.

A branch cracked to my left. Deliberate. He was herding me.

I veered right, laughing as I leaped over a fallen log. The forest blurred past, but my enhanced vision tracked every detail. The spider webs that trembled at my passing. The small creatures that fled our passage. The way moonlight reached for us between branches.

Then—impact.

He struck from above, his body wrapping around mine as we crashed to the ground. The landing should have hurt, but my body absorbed it, rolled with it, even as his weight pinned me into the earth. He seized my wrists above my head, and his teeth found the shell of my ear.

"Caught you," he growled, and I could hear his smile. His claws traced over my skin, and where once there might have been pain, all I felt was elation. The last shreds of my clothing tore away. I struggled against his hold, but he kept me firmly pinned, one hand sliding down my spine. As he passed over each vertebra, I felt them pop, my whole body straining to grow into something longer.

"My beautiful neidr."

With one swift motion, he flipped me onto my back, his hands gliding down to spread my legs. I pressed my palms into the forest floor, feeling the earth pulse beneath me. His weight shifted, and I heard the soft clicking of his additional limbs adjusting their hold.

He leaned back, releasing me. "Time for you to understand the monster you've awakened."

He began to shift, his legs merging into that huge, armored thorax, his chest broadening even further. The thick muscles of his arms twitched as his fingers elongated with sick, wet pops. I watched him transform, unsurprised to find that his true form only made me want him more.

"Why look at me like you're scared?" His face split apart as his mandibles emerged. "You love me pushing you to your limits, seeing just how strong you've become. Knowing I could break you, but that you can take so much more."

He was right. I struck, faster than I could comprehend. I was on him, and despite his massive size, I felt my body growing to match it. My fingers screamed in pain as they lengthened into knotted digits capped with claws—straight, razor-sharp, iridescent in the moonlight. My spine cracked as I grew taller, becoming something far beyond human.

We struggled with a force that would have shattered mortal bones. My claws carved furrows into the earth as I twisted beneath him. His spider limbs gouged deep trenches as he fought to pin me, ancient roots snapping like brittle reeds under our combined strength.

A young oak groaned and toppled when I slammed him against it, the trunk splintering from the impact. He retaliated by driving me through a wall of undergrowth, branches exploding around us in a shower of leaves and broken wood. The forest floor churned to mud beneath our thrashing bodies.

We were no longer human and spider, but two forces of nature colliding—and such forces always left destruction in their wake. I knocked him onto his back, all his limbs curling upward, and he laughed that deep, slow laugh.

"Yes, that's it. Show me everything you've become."

My pale skin was changing, my scarred flesh replaced by scales the color of moonlight. My tongue flicked out, and I tasted him—his excitement, his hunger, and bone-deep pride. They merged within me as I wrapped my much larger hands around his throat.

"Do you wish to devour me?" His grin widened. His arousal filled the air, but there was no fear.

I locked my legs around his waist, muscles bunching.

Yes, I wanted to crush him.

Yes, I wanted to consume him.

He was mine—my guardian, my creator, and my monster.

But now I was one too, and I didn't want to fear that part of myself.

I slammed my mouth to his and rolled my core against the ribbed surface of his thorax where it merged with the more human part of his body. Sparks of pleasure lit through me as each ridge dragged across my already throbbing clit.

Then the armor beneath me split.

The two heads of his fully monstrous cocks emerged—nothing like before. Earlier they had been mostly human, large but familiar in shape despite their number. This was not that.

My mouth watered as they emerged, a dark pink that bordered on purple, the heads sharp and slightly curved like his claws. The shafts twisted like the vines of the forest, every inch covered in tiny, spine-like protrusions.

He wrapped his large hand around them, spreading the

two lengths with a finger between. They were already slick with whatever fluid had kept them protected inside his body.

"I told you—you can't run from me now." He dragged a hand down one long shaft, and the base throbbed, swelling. "I'll knot inside you, and we'll be connected in a way most would not survive. Are you ready?"

I didn't hesitate. Every part of me craved him, wanted to feel exactly what he would be like. Preparation was not something this new body required. In fact, I clenched at the thought of any pain that might accompany the pleasure.

I ran my cunt over him, feeling those small spikes catch— just enough of a sting to stimulate, not enough to make me pull away.

"Ysu..." The next words died on my tongue. I couldn't say them, but I could show him, claim him with my body even if my voice failed me.

At the sound of his name, the hunger in his eyes softened. He leaned forward, wrapping multiple arms around me.

His lips found mine, gentler this time, his tongue sweeping over my lips, asking for that final permission. I opened for him, opened what I could of myself. The curved tips of his cocks pressed just slightly against both of my entrances, the larger testing the tightness of my ass.

But I wasn't afraid.

I wanted it all.

I sank down, the slick mixture of his precum and fluids easing him into me. There was a deep burn as I spread for him —but just as my spine and legs had grown to match his strength, the deepest part of me changed as well, reshaping to fit him.

The hunger in me had grown to mirror the hunger in him, and we had finally found a way to satiate it.

"My neidr." His eyes rolled back with a guttural groan as I took every inch of his length into both my ass and cunt. His body heated like it had after his massacre, his heart pounding erratically against my chest. "Mine. Only mine."

I rose and drove back down, filled so perfectly. Each stroke dragged those spines along my inner walls until my whole body buzzed, the twist of his shafts adding a delicious, unpredictable pleasure.

Then we were both lost to the hunger. More trees fell as he slammed me against them, wood splintering with every thrust. Teeth and tongues clashed; claws and hands gripped every part of me. My fangs traced the still-soft flesh of his neck, my split tongue following the dark markings there. The hunger in me twisted into pleasure so immense it threatened to break my mind when it finally crested.

My back hit the soft earth as he rutted into me—and then the burning returned as his knots began to swell, stretching me beyond what our bond could bear. I sank my claws into his shoulders, the pain finally overwhelming me.

"You were made for this, my neidr. Made for me." He ran his tongue along my jaw, licking up sweat and tears. "Let me knot your perfect cunt and ass, fill you to bursting, and let the whole world know you are mine and mine alone."

"Yes! Ysu, please!" I had said I wouldn't beg again, but I needed him now like I had never needed anything before.

I needed his strength, his endurance. I needed to give him everything I had and for him not to flinch. I needed to know he would never fear the monster I was, but would revel in it.

"Come with me, my neidr."

I cried out as he stilled, his knots swelling until I was sure he would rip me open. I felt him pulse inside me over and over, and even his knots couldn't keep all the cum he poured into me contained. The bulge in my stomach grew, and every bit of me was overwhelmed as that dark hunger consumed it all. My vision tunneled to nothing but the glow of his eyes as I came, clenching down on him even tighter, holding him close the way he had always held me.

Mine.

The word ghosted over my lips, a sacred vow. But as the world unraveled around me, unmade by the waves of pleasure still racking through me, I knew I wasn't that monster yet. I was incomplete, and my human heart was the coldest thing of all.

When I slowly returned to myself, I found Ysu watching me with an expression I couldn't read. His claws traced down my back and brushed my sweat-soaked hair from my face with exceptional gentleness.

I smiled, and my heart broke a little at the affection that lit his eight eyes. I pressed soft kisses across his cheeks—no biting, no claws. A silent plea for forgiveness. That I still wasn't strong enough to give him the one thing he truly needed. That he saw all of me and accepted it, while I couldn't voice what lived in my heart. Not yet.

We were still knotted together, so he wove a web to support me as he curled around my body. I rested against his chest as my transformation slowly receded, exhaustion finally overtaking me. He kissed my forehead with such tenderness, cradling me as he always did, keeping me safe.

And I had the terrible realization that I might be more of a monster than he was.

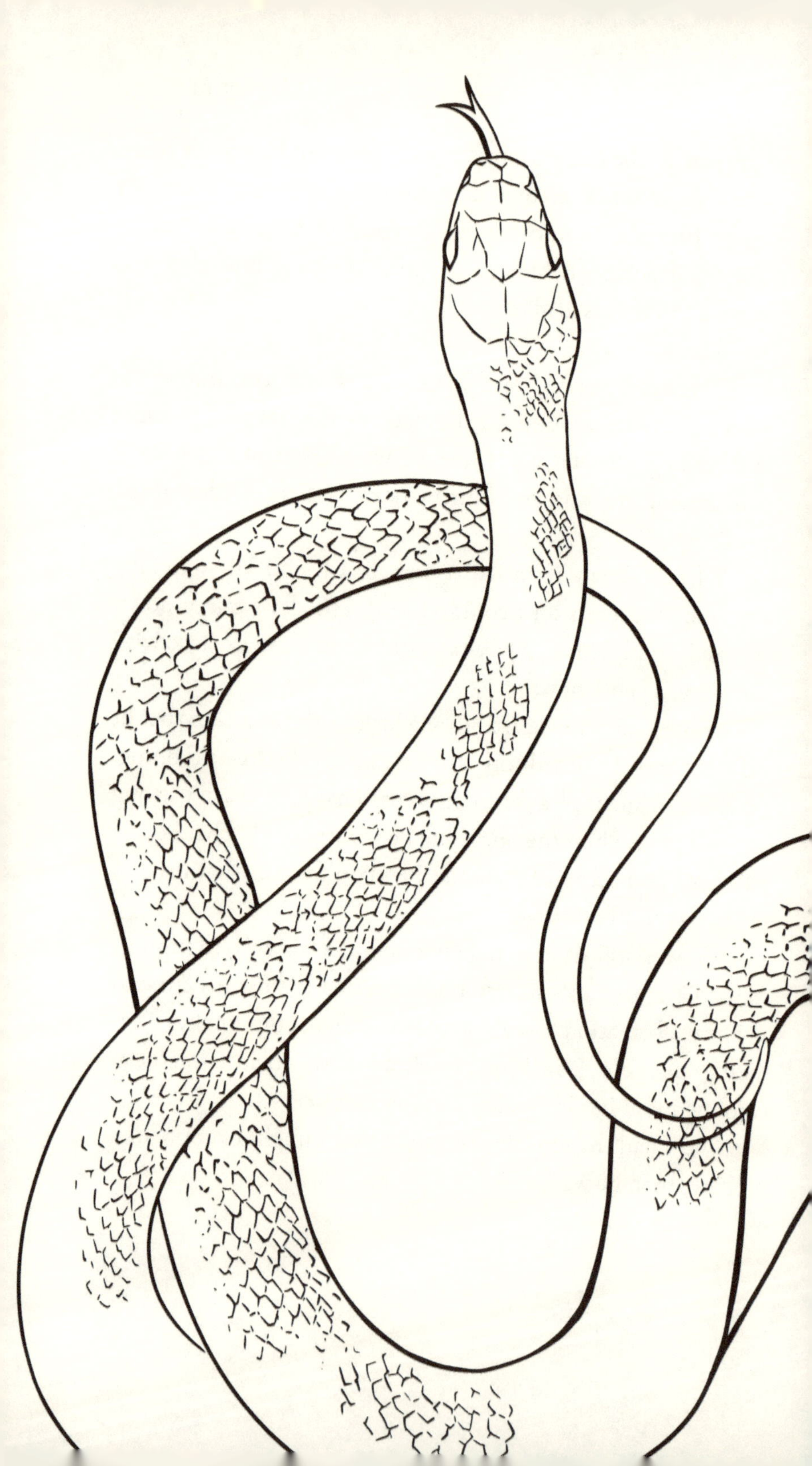

CHAPTER 15

FLAVIA

The scent hit me before the sound—wild rosemary mixed with old blood and something that spoke of transformation. My tongue flicked out involuntarily, tasting the air as Ysu's massive form stiffened beside me.

"We are not alone," he murmured, though his tone suggested he'd known long before I sensed anything.

Through the pre-dawn mist came footsteps, unhurried and unafraid. The figure that emerged from between the ancient oaks moved with lupine grace. A woman, tall and scarred, with hair the color of dried blood woven into complex braids. But it was her eyes that made my breath catch—golden, with pupils that narrowed to vertical slits when they found mine.

"Sister," she said in the old tongue, and the word resonated through my bones like a struck bell.

Ysu's chittering filled the grove, a warning of violence. His arms spread wide in a threat display. "This is my territory, wolf-child. You trespass."

The woman—though perhaps that word no longer fully applied—smiled, revealing canines that belonged in no human mouth. "Peace, ancient one. I come not for your web or prey, only for the newly born." Her golden gaze returned to me. "The deep forest calls its children home. The guardians gather at the new moon to discuss the Roman plague."

"She goes nowhere." Ysu moved between us, his form expanding until he loomed over the wolf-woman. "The serpent is mine."

"Is she marked?" The woman tilted her head, nostrils flaring as she emphasized the word. "I smell only venom and pleasure, spider. No true claim the forest would recognize."

The grove exploded into motion. Ysu struck with all his arms at once, but the wolf-woman flowed around his attacks like water. She moved on all fours now, her form blurring between human and beast with each leap. Their battle carved gouges in ancient trees and sent birds screaming from their roosts. The spiders at Ysu's command stirred the forest floor, trying to climb her, but she shook them off.

"Stop!" My voice rang clear, and both combatants froze mid-strike. The serpent in my belly uncoiled, tasting the violence in the air with appreciation. "I am not a bone to be fought over by scavengers."

The wolf-woman laughed, a sound like wind through mountain passes. "Well spoken, sister. You see? She has her own voice. The forest chooses well."

"The forest." Ysu's mandibles clicked with barely contained rage. "Always the forest. As if trees and soil have precedence over the one who gave her new life." He turned to me, all eight eyes blazing with an intensity I hadn't seen before. "Tell her, my neidr. Tell her who you belong to."

The words hung between us like a challenge—and a plea. I felt the answer lodged in my chest, words I wanted to speak but couldn't force past the wall of my own terror. Simple words that would have eased the anguish twisting his face.

But I couldn't.

"I belong to myself," I answered instead.

The truth was more complicated. Part of me did belong to him—the part that had learned to trust, that had discovered strength in his patient teaching, that craved his embrace. But another part remembered what belonging had meant before.

I wanted to be Ysu's. Wanted to claim him in return. But every time I tried, my throat closed. My mind filled with echoes of Tiberius saying *mine*, of centurions dividing me between them like spoils of war, of years when claiming meant nothing but pain.

"Not enough." The words tore from Ysu, broken and desperate. He reached for me with shaking hands, pulling me against his chest, his grip crushing.

"The wolf is correct," he said. "The forest will continue to call you, to try to claim you for itself. It would use you, as it has used me. It recognizes no one-sided oaths or promises. It speaks only in the language of the old magic, a language written in blood."

The pull I'd been fighting for days flared. The forest's ancient hunger reaching through my blood, whispering promises of power, of belonging to something vast and timeless. It had been growing stronger, and I realized now why Ysu had grown increasingly desperate.

The wolf-woman nodded as the wind picked up, whipping my hair across my face. "The forest can no longer wait. It calls upon the debt your blood owes."

"What debt?" I asked, but Ysu's arms tightened around me, and my feet left the ground.

"Her debt is to me now, wolf. The forest may not recognize oaths, but it will recognize that which is written in flesh."

I stiffened.

"Ysu, don't..."

"I'm sorry, my neidr," he rasped, desperation bleeding into his voice. "The forest will never stop calling you, not until it has driven you mad. I would not have this place become your prison, as it is mine."

I felt the truth in his words, felt the forest's patient malevolence pressing at the edges of my mind. But despite the ancient magics gathering around us, all I could think of were laughing faces as my flesh was torn apart.

"Don't, please..." *Don't make me see* him *when I look at you.* It came out as a sob, but he didn't stop.

His fangs found the juncture of my neck and shoulder, piercing deep. I felt the pulse of his venom as it flowed into me. But this was different from before—not a hunt, but a claiming. It moved under my skin as if it had a will of its own.

Markings bloomed across my skin—black lines tracing from throat to collarbone, a mirror of his web. I squirmed, but he held me tight, and I was still too weak to overcome him, especially with my heart breaking.

The forest's call dimmed, its hold loosening as something stronger took precedence.

When Ysu pulled back, there was no cruelty in his gaze, but triumph shone in all eight eyes. "Now any who look upon you will know. The forest may try to call you, but I claimed you first."

The wolf-woman watched with an expression caught between amusement and pity. "The spider shows his true nature at last. Driven to madness, as the old stories warned." She shook her head, braids swaying. "Keep your bride, then, weaver. But know this—when the stones sing and the moon darkens, she will be needed. War will come for us all, no matter your allegiance."

She turned to leave, then paused. "Sister," she called to me. "When you tire of silk chains and pretty scars, remember you have kin who understand the burden of transformation. We gather at the standing stones when his grip grows too tight."

Then she was gone, melting into the forest. Ysu's arms remained locked around me, his breathing gradually slowing from combat-readiness to something more controlled.

I reached up, tracing the new marks on my skin, feeling how they pulsed with his venom—his claim. A mark of ownership, one I had sworn I would never allow again.

CHAPTER 16

FLAVIA

He loosened his grip, and I flung myself away. "Don't." The word came out sharper than any fang. "Don't touch me."

"Neidr—"

"No." I stood, putting distance between us, my hand pressed to the fresh marks burned into my skin. The black lines pulsed with his venom, and each throb sent waves of rage through me I could barely contain.

"Do you know what you've done?" My voice cracked on the words, fury and heartbreak warring in my chest. "Do you even understand?"

His multiple eyes blinked in sequence, and for once he seemed uncertain. "I claimed you. Protected you from the forest's call."

"You marked me!" The rage that had been building exploded outward, shaking the very air around us. "Years. Years I spent being scarred for someone else's pleasure, someone else's need to own and control. And the first time another of my kind appears—when anything threatens your control—you do the same thing."

The words tasted bitter, like betrayal. Because beneath the fury was something worse: I had begun to believe he was different. To trust that the gentleness he'd shown me was real, that his protection came without the price of my freedom.

"It's not the same." His voice hardened, defensive. "I am not them. You came to me for protection. I have provided it."

"I came to you for revenge. Not to trade one master's knife for another's fangs." I backed farther away as he stood, his form towering in the dim grove. "She called them pretty scars. Pretty. Like decorations. Like I'm your property to mark as you see fit."

The truth sat like a stone in my chest. Part of me understood why he'd done it. I had felt forest's pull, its desire for power above all else. But understanding didn't heal the wound of betrayal, didn't erase the sick familiarity of waking up with new scars.

"You *are* mine." The words burst from him with enough force to shake the trees. "You swore it. Mind, body, soul—"

"I lied. I intended to die."

He froze. "You never intended to be mine." I saw him break then, saw the realization crash over him—that in trying to keep me, he had driven me away. But I couldn't stop, couldn't hold back the poison that had been building in my chest.

"You once called me pathetic. And you were right. When I came to you, I was desperate. But even in my pathetic state, I promised myself I would never let anyone own me again."

He moved closer, and I could see the possessive madness in all eight eyes. "Three hundred years I have been a slave to hunger, to this ancient curse. But it wasn't until I met you that

I understood unending desire—need so deep that I sometimes fear it will unravel the very threads of my existence. No matter your intention, you are mine, neidr. I cannot let you go."

There was raw pain in his voice, and it called to something deep in my chest. The part of me that had found safety in his arms, that had seen beauty in his monstrous form, that had begun to imagine a future shared between two creatures of hunger and rage.

But that future lay in ashes now, burned by his inability to trust that I would stay without chains.

"You were going to kill me when we first met," I said, forcing steel into my voice. "To devour me. Don't lie to me about what you are."

"You came seeking a monster," he replied, deadly quiet. "And now you are surprised you found one?"

The marks on my neck continued to throb. "No. Only that I thought he might understand me."

The corners of his eyes softened. "My neidr..."

But I was already running.

The forest blurred past as I pushed my new body to its limits. I heard him crashing through the trees behind me.

I didn't care. The wound at my throat throbbed with each heartbeat, his venom ensuring it would scar exactly as he intended. Another chain. Another reminder that my body would never truly be my own.

The trees began to thin, and I realized I'd run farther than ever before. The edge of his territory. The boundary of his web's influence. One more step and I would be in truly wild forest, completely on my own.

I stopped at the invisible line, breathing hard. Not from exertion—my transformed body could run for hours—but from the weight of choice. Behind me lay Ysu's grove, his obsessive protection, his suffocating need. Ahead lay the unknown: others like me who might understand the changes I was just starting to accept.

The marks pulsed, reminding me of venom in my veins, of promises made under blood moons, of the terrible intimacy we'd shared. He was right about one thing—he was in my blood now. Part of me in ways that went beyond the physical.

But that didn't mean I had to accept his chains. I'd made a promise to him, but he had always known the truth: humans lie. And I was still human—at least a small part of me. And I had made a promise to myself first.

I took one step across the boundary. Then another. Each movement away from his web felt like tearing silk, like breaking something woven into my very essence. But I kept walking, even as the forest around me changed—older, stranger, less familiar.

Let him rage. Let him hunt. I would not be anyone's pretty prize, marked and displayed for ownership. Not anymore. Not even for the monster who'd saved me, who I thought I had maybe...

I shook my head, banishing the thought. No going back now.

The wolf-woman had spoken of standing stones. It was time to learn what I could be without Ysu's shadow defining my every step.

Behind me, the forest shivered with his devastation.

But I didn't look back.

CHAPTER 17

FLAVIA

The wolf-woman found me by a stream at dawn, trying to wash Ysu's scent from my skin.

"Three days," she observed, settling on a boulder with lupine grace. "Longer than I expected. I thought you would have gone back by now."

I scrubbed harder at my arms, watching dirt swirl away in the current. "I'm not crawling back."

"No?" She tilted her head, golden eyes bright with amusement. "Yet you wear his mark like a collar, little sister. Pretty black scars for a pretty pet."

I snarled at her. "He had no right—"

"Rights?" Her laugh was wild as a winter storm. "You speak of rights in the old forest? Here there is only power and choice. You chose him. He chose to mark you. Now you choose whether to accept it or claw it off." She leaned forward. "Though I should warn you, some scars are not so easily removed."

I abandoned my futile washing, sitting back on my heels. The forest around us breathed differently than Ysu's grove—

older, less ordered, full of watchful shadows that held no loyalty.

"What do you want?" I asked, not bothering to temper my voice with kindness.

She leaned against a nearby tree, legs and arms crossed casually. "I came to make sure you were alright out here on your own. Not many things can survive in these old woods, even things like us."

"Out of the kindness of your heart?" The sarcasm was thick.

She grinned, and it was completely wolf. "You are strong, sister. That much is apparent. The forest needs you—we need you. But I don't come empty-handed."

"Maybe I'm tired of bargains." I stood, facing her. I was surprised to find I was taller than she was.

Her grin didn't falter. "Think of it as a gift, then. There are abilities your spider never showed you. Magic your serpent gift grants you. To stare into the eyes of your prey and control their mind."

Her casual tone made my skin crawl—the dismissive ease with which she spoke about Ysu.

"Would he have known this?" My heart thumped, thinking Ysu might have kept something from me, withheld it to keep me weak. I hated how much the thought hurt. I shouldn't have cared that he had kept things from me. He was a monster...and yet I had let myself believe he might not be what the stories said he was. That perhaps he had truly cared for me, in his own broken way.

The wolf-woman looked thoughtful. "Perhaps not. The spider has always kept to his domain, not interacting with us. He has never met another serpent before."

Another serpent. Someone like me. "But you have?"

"Yes." Something devious returned to her eyes. "There is much I could show you."

The gleam in her gaze made the truth snap into place. "You knew this would happen," I said suddenly. "When you spoke to Ysu. You knew he would react. That he might mark me."

Her expression didn't change, but her scent shifted—amusement mixed with something sharper. "The spider has always been a romantic. A possessive creature. It took very little to remind him of what he feared most." She was utterly unapologetic.

"And what was that?" I asked.

She looked at me as though the answer was obvious. "Losing you, of course."

Heat flared in my chest, rage awakening the serpent within. "You manipulated him. Manipulated both of us."

"I offered truth. What he chose to do with it was his own failing." She shrugged, unconcerned. "The forest needs you, serpent. Your spider's attachments were...inconvenient."

Inconvenient. Everything we'd shared, reduced to an obstacle in whatever agenda she carried.

Yes, he had marked me without permission. Yes, he had claimed ownership in a way that echoed too closely my years with Tiberius. But unlike my Roman captors, Ysu had also held me through nightmares. Had taught me to see strength where I saw only scars. Had looked at me not as something broken to be used, but as something powerful waiting to emerge.

"He always gave me a choice," I said quietly, more to myself than to her. "Even when he was never given one."

Her laugh was sharp. "How touching. But sentiment won't serve you in what's to come. The forest has plans, and you need proper instruction. Your spider taught you to wait and strike, but serpents are so much more than that. Let me show you how to truly hunt—"

"No." The word came out harsher than I intended, surprising us both. I straightened, feeling something settle into place inside me. "I won't be anyone's tool again. Not Ysu's, not the forest's, and certainly not yours."

Her eyes narrowed. "You're being foolish. Alone, you're vulnerable. Your transformation is incomplete, and there are abilities you don't even know exist—"

"Then I'll learn them myself." I turned toward the deeper woods, away from both her and the direction of Ysu's grove. "I don't need anyone telling me what I should become."

"You'll fail without guidance. The serpent's call requires understanding, finesse—"

"I said no." I met her gaze directly. Then I stopped hiding.

Joints popped as I grew even taller, and my nails extended. Her features shifted as my vision caught the heat of her, and I watched with delight as her heart began to race.

For a moment, I thought she might fight me—force me. But she only grunted and turned away with a gesture that somehow managed to be both dismissive and approving.

"Your funeral, serpent. Don't come crying to me when you're starving and lost."

She walked away without looking back.

My body shrank again, unable to hold the extended form. I shivered as scales sank back beneath my skin. I rubbed my arms, cold and overwhelmed by the vast, open future before me.

Then my stomach growled, loudly. It had been days since I had eaten. My future could wait. For now, the hunt called.

The deeper woods were quieter, older. Here the trees grew so thick that afternoon looked like twilight. I found a small clearing where rabbits grazed and settled at the edge, trying to remember everything Ysu had taught me.

Patience, his voice echoed in my memory. *Observe first. Understand your prey before you act.*

I watched the rabbits for a long time, noting how they moved, where they felt safe, which ones were young and inexperienced. Ysu had always emphasized this—the importance of reading a situation fully before committing to action. He'd taught me to see patterns, to understand the subtle signs that meant the difference between success and failure.

Feel what you are, I remembered him saying during one of our lessons. *Don't fight the serpent. Let it guide you.*

I let my breathing slow and allowed that coiled presence beneath my skin to unfurl. The world sharpened around me—scents clearer, sounds more distinct—and I could sense the warm pulse of life from the rabbits across the clearing.

One young buck had wandered slightly apart from the others. I focused on him, trying to understand what the wolf-woman had meant about calling with my eyes. At first nothing happened. The rabbit continued nibbling tender shoots, oblivious to me.

Then I remembered something else Ysu had taught me—not about hunting, but about connection. How he said the venom had recognized something in my blood, something that called to his own darkness. Perhaps this calling wasn't about force, but about finding that thread of recognition between predator and prey.

I thought of the rabbit's warm blood, the quick flutter of his heart. I remembered what it felt like to be small and vulnerable, always listening for danger, always ready to run. And then I imagined the relief of not having to run anymore. The peace of surrender.

The rabbit's head rose slowly. His dark eyes found mine, and for a moment that stretched like cold honey, we simply looked at each other. I felt something pass between us—not magic exactly, but understanding. An acknowledgment of what we both were.

Come, I thought, not as command but as invitation. *Come and find your rest.*

He took one hesitant step toward me. Then another. His body trembled with the wrongness of it, but his eyes never left mine. Each step was a choice, even as some deeper part of him had already surrendered to the inevitable, to the cycle that would eventually consume us both.

When he was close enough to touch, I moved quickly and cleanly, the way Ysu had shown me. One swift motion, and it was over. The rabbit went limp in my hands, his suffering ended before it could begin. I hadn't wanted him to feel fear— only surrender.

Respect your prey, Ysu had always said. *And honor the life that sustains you.*

I whispered a small thanks to the rabbit's spirit before I fed. Taking life meant accepting responsibility for that sacrifice.

As I ate, I realized how much his patient instruction had shaped me. Not just the techniques, but the philosophy behind them. The idea that strength should be tempered with wisdom, that power required restraint. He had never once pushed me beyond what I was ready for, had always waited for me to choose each step forward.

His marks ached, but the pain felt different now. Less like chains, more like...a reminder. A connection to someone who had seen the predator in me before I could see it myself. Someone who had nurtured that darkness while teaching me to wield it.

I called two more rabbits that afternoon, growing more confident with each attempt. The serpent's call wasn't about domination—it was about offering a kind of peace, a release from the constant vigilance that marked a prey animal's existence. I released one of them, still filled from the first. I had power, but I chose when to use it. I was not a slave to the hunger within me.

As the sun dipped low, I settled against a tree trunk, belly full but heart strangely empty. The forest floor was hard without silk to cushion it, and every shadow held dangers I didn't yet know. But I had done this—learned and succeeded, using the foundation Ysu had given me to build something new.

He had taught me all I needed. Tears rose as I remembered how I had once believed he kept things from me to keep me weak. He never would have done that. He had done everything he could to help me transform, to become what I was meant to be.

As night and winter cold settled around me, I found no warm arms to hold me. The wind whipped the leaves, and I heard the forest's call. It was muffled, hidden beneath the thrum of Ysu's venom, but I still heard it. It offered purpose but no comfort. It required strength, but it had never held me when I was frightened.

I had choices to make. But alone on the cold ground, missing him more than I cared to admit, I wondered if freedom was worth the price of solitude.

Somewhere in the distance, a wolf howled—lonely despite the pack that surrounded her. And from another direction, carried on the night wind, came the faint song of webs vibrating in an empty grove.

Chapter 18

Flavia

The standing stones sang at midnight.

I woke on the cold forest floor, their resonance thrumming through my bones with a vibration that seemed to rise from the earth itself. With no silk to cushion me, it was mind-numbing. Just earth and stone and the deep pull of ancient magic calling me.

I wandered into the woods until I recognized the wolf-woman's scent.

She emerged from the shadows, her golden eyes already open and alert. "You hear them."

"Yes." I stood beside her, fingers drifting unconsciously to the black web of scars. They tingled with each pulse of the stones' song—Ysu's lingering claim resisting that ancient magic. "Growing louder."

"Growing impatient." She shook leaves from her hair. "The forest won't wait much longer."

She paused. "I am sorry for my...cruelty before. I have not dealt with someone as human as you in many years. I forgot the wildness of the forest has not hardened you yet."

Not much of an apology.

"I can scent the harm you have undergone. I am transformed, just as you are. I walked a path similar to yours many years ago. I should have been more mindful," she continued. "I hope we can run as sisters, despite my misstep."

It wasn't enough, not yet. But as the forest's call nearly drowned out all other thought, this wasn't the time to discuss manners among monsters.

"What is your name?" I asked.

She blinked, surprised. "Names are not so commonly used among our kind."

I bit my lip. There was so much I still had to learn.

"But you may call me Cysgod, if you like."

I nodded. She turned away, her braids swaying, and I saw the scar on the back of her neck. A bite mark I knew went deep.

"Did you have a..." My eyes lingered on the scar.

"A demon of my own?" Her gaze twinkled with something sharp. "Yes, but a long time has passed since then. Perhaps a story for another time. Right now, you have a choice to make."

I looked at this woman touched by the spirit of a wolf and saw one path. I looked back toward Ysu's domain and saw another. But the future was like a spider's web—fractured into infinite possibilities. I didn't know where I would end up, but I knew I could no longer linger in idleness. I needed to take a step, any step, forward.

I wrapped my arms around myself against the night's chill and shivered uncontrollably. In Ysu's grove, I'd never felt cold like this.

"Will he be there?" The question escaped before I could stop it.

Cysgod's smile held too much knowledge. "The spider is

the oldest of us all. He rarely leaves his web. Too proud. Too afraid someone might steal what he considers his." She tilted her head. "Does that disappoint you, little sister?"

I didn't answer, but the fresh scars pulsed, as if curious for the truth. Part of me hoped he would come—would see me standing among the others, an equal. Another part feared what would happen if he did.

Cysgod led the way with serene confidence, her pack of wolves flowing around us like gray ghosts. They accepted me, these wild hunters, though I caught them watching me with wary curiosity.

The stones stood in a clearing that felt older than Rome, older than human memory. Thirteen monoliths arranged in a perfect circle, each twice the height of a man and carved with spirals and symbols whose meaning had long since been worn away. Mortal eyes would miss the patterns, but mine were no longer mortal, and I saw how the carvings breathed with power that made even Ysu's ancient web feel young by comparison.

We were not the first to arrive.

At the northern stone stood others: a bark-skinned man whose fingers coiled like ancient roots; twins with vulpine grace and amber eyes that glimmered with sly intelligence as they circled the stones.

And at the southern stone—

"Sister!" A voice rang with delight as another serpent-touched woman emerged from the shadows. Her transformation was further along than mine—scales covered half her face, and when she smiled, her jaw unhinged slightly. "Oh, they said you might come! The youngest of us. How brave."

"Adda," Cysgod said. "She is also serpent-blessed, claimed by the forest fifty winters past."

Fifty winters. I studied the woman who might be my

future, noting how she moved—always flowing, never quite still. Her eyes held depths that spoke of decades spent more snake than human. But there was something else there too: a power that called to the magic inside me like a beacon.

"And still sane," Adda added, reading my thoughts with eerie ease. "Though sanity, sweet sister, is a flexible concept when you've swallowed men whole and felt their last thoughts dissolve in your belly." She circled me slowly, nostrils flaring. "You smell of spider silk and sorrow. He marked you deep, didn't he?"

Her expression softened. "I had one too, once. A guardian who thought to keep me. But serpents aren't meant for webs, little sister. We're meant to move, to flow, to swallow the world one piece at a time."

Around us, others gathered—shifting shapes, hybrid creatures touched by ancient spirits. And behind them, great guardians watched from the forest's edge: a bear with eyes like stars, a wolf the size of a horse—whose gaze lingered on Cysgod—and near the eastern stones, a stag whose antlers glowed like dying star.

These were the true guardians, the first to answer the forest's call. Ysu's kin, though he stayed away.

"The children gather," Cysgod announced. "The moon wanes. The Romans mass their forces to the south, planning to burn what they cannot conquer. The forest has been patient. The forest has waited. But now—"

The stones flared with cold light, and suddenly I understood. The patterns carved into them weren't decorative—they were a map. A living representation of the land itself, showing Roman settlements as infected wounds and their roads like scars. It showed their steady advance into territories that had been wild since the world began. The wind rose and I heard the forest whisper, *We are the same, you and I. They have marked us, scarred us, but we will not bow, and we will not break.*

"Now we take back what is ours," Adda hissed, her voice echoing with the hiss of a thousand serpents. "But first, youngest sister, you must complete your becoming."

"I've transformed," I said, though even as the words left my mouth, I knew they were only half-truths.

"Partially." Adda moved closer, and I could smell old blood on her breath—decades of hunts. "You've let spider venom change you, yes. You hunt, you feed, but you have not claimed your birthright fully. You have not completed the cycle."

Understanding crashed through me like ice water. "Tiberius."

"The one who first broke you. The one whose cruelty opened the door for transformation." Cysgod stepped forward. "You must consume the source of your pain to truly become. Only then will you be complete enough to serve in the war to come."

I felt suddenly, desperately alone as every eye in the grove fixed on me. If Ysu were here, he would rage at them for suggesting I serve anyone but him. He would wrap me in his possessive fury and block out everything but his presence. I would have pressed my face into his chest as he kept the world from touching me.

But he wasn't here, and I had chosen that.

"I left him to rot," I explained. "Bound in web and madness. He is dead already."

Adda shook her head. "Finish what you started, sister. You must complete this curse if you are ever to be free."

From the circle's center, the earth began to crack. What emerged wasn't quite mist, wasn't quite light, but something between—the forest's will made visible. It touched each of us in turn, and where it passed, transformations accelerated. The bark-skinned man groaned as roots burst from his flesh. The twins fell to all fours as their forms locked into massive fox shapes.

When it reached me, the pain was exquisite.

My spine elongated with audible pops. Scales erupted across my skin in waves, each a small agony that built into a transcendent sensation. I felt my jaw restructuring, bone reshaping to accommodate the unhinging motion I'd only imitated before. The serpent in my belly became my belly, became my entire being.

But this time, no strong arms caught me as I convulsed. No familiar presence anchored me through the pain. I writhed alone on cold ground while the forest worked its will through my flesh, and I understood with cold lucidity the price of the freedom I'd claimed.

When the light faded, I lay gasping on earth that felt too solid, too limiting. My body had returned mostly to human shape, unable to hold the transformation. But I could feel the potential coiled within—the full serpent waiting to emerge when I claimed my final prey.

Soon, the forest whispered through stone and soil. *Soon you will be ready. The circle must close.*

Adda helped me stand, her touch gentle despite her monstrous strength. "The transformation is not easy," she said quietly. "It's never easy. But we endure, little sister. We serpents always endure."

Around us, the other chosen began to disperse, returning to their territories to prepare for the battle the stones had shown was coming. I stood on shaking legs, feeling more unsure than I had since that first night in Ysu's grove.

"Where will you go?" Cysgod asked.

I touched my neck, feeling how the marks burned with my transformation, how they called to their maker even across the distance between us. The forest had shown me my path—back to the villa, back to Tiberius, back to the completion of what I'd started.

It had shown me revenge centuries in the making, of expelling the men who thought to claim and tame something beautiful and wild. I understood that rage well, and I shared the forest's wounds.

But my mind kept drifting back to the spider who'd helped make me. Who had seen me before I became something strong.

Would he still have me? Could I bear to return?

The stones fell silent, but their promise echoed in my bones: *Complete the cycle. Consume the source. Become.*

And in the cold darkness, with no web to catch me, I stood at a crossroads. My future was my own, and I had to decide what I wanted to make of it.

CHAPTER 19

FLAVIA

I found him in the darkest part of his grove, where the web was woven thick enough to block out the stars. He sat perfectly still on the ancient stump he'd claimed as his throne, all eight eyes closed, his form so motionless he might have been carved from stone.

"I know you're there," he said without opening his eyes. "I've tasted your approach in my web for the last hour."

I stepped into the grove proper, noting how the silk no longer sang at my presence. It hung neutral—neither welcoming nor warning. Just...indifferent. The realization made my stomach drop.

"I went to the stones."

"Obviously." He opened his primary eyes, the others remaining shut. "You smell of their magic." His mandibles clicked once, sharp. "And of the wolf-woman's mutts."

"Are you going to ask me why I came back?"

"No." He rose with that terrible grace but didn't approach. "I know why you came back. The stones told you what must be done. Complete the cycle. Consume your tormentor.

Become." Each word fell like ice. "You need to reach the villa. Pass through my territory."

I moved closer, but he shifted away, maintaining the distance between us. "That's not the only reason," I replied.

His laugh held no warmth. "Tell me, neidr, what other reason could there be? You made your position quite clear when you ran. You were never mine—only desperate. A slave to a new master."

"I was angry—"

"You were honest. Perhaps the most honest you've ever been with me." He turned his back to me, something he'd never done before. "And perhaps correct. I marked you without permission. Claimed you without consent. Bound you with scars you'll carry forever." His additional arms unfurled from beneath his robe, gesturing to the empty grove. "So take what you need. The path to the villa is clear. Complete your transformation. Become what you're meant to be."

"You're dismissing me?"

"I'm freeing you." He still wouldn't look at me. "Isn't that what you wanted? Freedom from my web? Space to discover what you are without me defining your every step?"

The marks on my neck throbbed, the venom longing to come home. "Then why does it feel like punishment?"

He whirled, all eight eyes open and blazing. "Punishment? You think this is punishment?" His form expanded, revealing the monstrous truth beneath his controlled exterior. "Punishment would be binding you in silk until you remembered who you belong to. Punishment would be hunting down every creature that dared call you sister and hanging their husks from my web. Punishment would be keeping you here, caged in my grove, until the stars burned out rather than let you walk away again."

"Then why don't you?"

The question hung between us. When he answered, his voice was quiet again, carefully controlled. "Because you were right. About the marking." He touched his own chest, where dark markings mimicked mine. "I swore to protect you. That you wouldn't suffer as you had before. Then at the first challenge to my claim, I carved into you like...like I didn't believe you would stay without it."

"Ysu—"

"Go." The word cracked in his chest. "Hunt your tormentor. Complete your gods-damned cycle. But don't—" He paused, and for a moment something raw crossed his expression. "Don't pretend you came back for anything more than passage."

"Stop it." The words came out weighted with tears.

"Stop what? Speaking truth? You missed comfort, perhaps. Protection. The certainty of my web." He gestured dismissively. "Any guardian could provide that. The wolf seems eager to collect strays."

"The wolf doesn't see me as I am—only what I'm becoming."

"And I do?" He moved then, circling me while still keeping his distance. "I understand hunger. Possession. The need to clutch at beautiful things until they break. But understanding you? No, neidr. I never understood you. I only wanted to keep you."

"Liar. You knew when I needed to be pushed and when I needed to be held. You helped me be strong and cradled me so I could surrender. You stopped my nightmares. You...cared for me."

He stopped circling. "What would you have me say? That I still want you? That every hour you were gone felt like centuries? That I've been sitting here forcing myself not to hunt you down and drag you back?" His voice dropped to barely above a whisper. "That letting you leave again might be the hardest thing I've done in my entire cursed life?"

"Then don't let me."

"And prove you right? That I'm just another chain?" He shook his head. "No. You want freedom? Take it. Take it and leave me to my endless hunger."

My heart ached, and I knew the truth—the truth I had been hiding from myself. Because deep down, I had never been as strong as he believed. I had always been a coward. I saw his pain, and still I couldn't bring forth the words that lingered in the last fragile part of me that was human.

"Your silence speaks volumes," he said softly. "So go. Become. But stop torturing us both with false promises."

"I never meant to hurt you."

He chuckled, but it held no humor. He finally turned to face me, reaching out, one claw ghosting over the marks on my neck without touching. "These scars bind you to me, yes. But chains work both ways, neidr. Every moment you're gone, I feel the pull. Every hour, I have to choose not to follow. Do you know what that costs?"

"Come with me. To the villa. Like you wanted to before—"

"No." He pulled back. "This is your hunt. Your choice." His next words were barely audible. "And when you're done, if you choose to return...then we'll discuss what we are to each other. But not before. Not with lies and half-truths and borrowed comfort masquerading as affection."

I stared at him, this ancient creature trying so hard to let me go, despite every instinct screaming otherwise. "You're afraid I won't come back."

"I'm certain you won't. Once you are complete, you will have no need of me." He turned away again. "The truth is, you were always strong. You never needed me. But that's my burden to bear, not yours. The path to the villa is clear. Hunt well."

"Ysu—"

"Go, my neidr. Please." The last word scraped raw, torn from somewhere deep. "Before I forget my resolve and do something else I cannot take back."

I stood there for a long moment, watching his rigid back, feeling the weight of everything unsaid between us. Then I turned and walked toward the villa, each step more painful than the last.

Behind me came the sound of silk tearing—Ysu destroying his own web rather than feel me walk across it.

The message was clear: I was free.

So why did it feel like everything was falling apart?

CHAPTER 20

FLAVIA

I left Ysu's grove with my heart heavy. He had spoken of desire for comfort masquerading as affection, but I knew that wasn't true. I did miss his web and his protection, yes —but because they were his. I missed the patterns he wove above my hammock, beauty he created just for me. I missed waking in the day to the sight of his slumbering face, softened without the harsh lines carved by unending hunger. Like being with me was enough. Like I allowed him some peace.

Tears rose in my eyes. He had seen me when I didn't deserve it. I had lied, I had been desperate, but he had claimed me all the same. As if I had been worthy. Perhaps I had been— but he had believed it first, and that had allowed me to believe it too.

And I had used him. Intended to renege on our bargain. I had come into the woods seeking a monster, when I had been one all along. I had used his power for my revenge, but when the strength and possessiveness that had drawn me to him slipped past his control, I fled.

He deserved better. He deserved to hear how I really felt, even if it didn't change what I needed to do.

I turned around, determined to return—but the forest had other plans. The path that should have led to him twisted back on itself, and mist rose from ground that had been dry moments before. The trees pressed closer, their branches forming a tunnel that led not toward home but deeper into the wild.

"Daughter."

I froze. That voice—soft, accented with the old tongue. My mother stood at the heart of a stone circle, but not as I remembered her. This was the woman she'd hidden: tall and proud, wearing robes that seemed woven from moonlight. Her hair, the same moon-pale shade as mine, writhed with its own life.

"You're dead," I said, though in this place the word held little meaning.

"Dead, alive—such limited concepts." She gestured, and I saw the truth written in the movement of her hands. "I am memory. I am bloodline. I am the curse trying to complete itself through you."

The scars at my throat pulsed, Ysu's venom still trying to protect me from the forest's manipulations. Her form wavered, but I gently traced the raised lines along my neck.

Let me hear her.

The scars quieted, but waited, watching closely.

The forest shifted around us, showing me visions from across time. My grandmother speaking words rooted in the heart of the wildwood. My great-grandmother offering sacrifices to spirits in exchange for the power to fight the invaders. Back and back, a chain of women who bargained with darkness until darkness became their blood. The woman before me was my mother, but she was also every woman who came before her. A chain of memory and burden stretching to the beginning of us all.

"Tell me." The words came out part hiss, part plea. "Tell me what you did."

She gestured, and the mist shaped itself into images. I saw a circle of women, naked beneath a blood moon, standing around stones that looked freshly carved.

"The Romans had burned the sacred groves. Salted the ritual grounds. Killed our druids." The image shifted, showing legions marching through forests that withered at their passage. "We were desperate. So we called to the heart of the forest, and it allowed us to reach into the spaces between —the void where the oldest spirits dwelt. We called them by their true names and offered them flesh anchors in our world."

"The guardians."

"They were not guardians then. They were...hunger. Pure appetite given form. The spider that weaves reality. The serpent that swallows suns. The wolf that runs between worlds." She shuddered, the terror of those ancient powers palpable. "We offered them human vessels in exchange for protecting the land. They accepted."

The mist shifted, showing the thirteen priestesses and the standing stones. Then, at the center, a man bound and gagged —a face I knew. Human then, but unmistakable. Dark hair hiding a sharp jaw, fear widening his eyes. He might be a monster now, but once he had been only a man, choice stripped away.

He struggled against his bindings as a priestess approached. She wore a robe that covered her head and a mask fashioned from a deer skull, its antlers reaching toward the sky. She held out her hand, slicing across her palm until blood dripped onto the forest floor. With that dark liquid, she traced whorls across his chest in before stepping back to join her sisters.

Their chant rose, resonating with chords that called to the world beyond. The ground cracked open, and a dark mist broke through like the hand of death. It had no true form—only a spirit of pure appetite. It writhed and reached with appendages extending in all directions, searching until it located its prey.

"You seek flesh," she said in the old tongue, her voice carrying power that shook the trees. "We offer anchors. Take this vessel, be bound to mortal form. But know this—as we give, so must you. Blood for blood, venom for venom." The spirit resisted until she drew her ritual blade across her palm, letting her blood drip onto the man who would become Ysu. The exchange was sealed—the spirit flowing into flesh, screaming as infinite hunger was compressed into finite form.

The mist shifted to new horrors—the spirits taking their first hosts, transforming them into things neither human nor beast. Villages emptied as people fled. The forest itself began to change, growing stranger and hungrier with each passing season.

"We summoned them, and then realized our folly." Her laugh was bitter. "The guardians were too powerful. We thought to control what cannot be controlled—just as arrogant as the Romans we fought."

"We won battles against our enemies, yes, but the spirits... they wanted more. Always more. They began taking whoever entered their domains, friend or foe. Creating armies of trans- formed humans to spread their influence."

"So you cursed them."

"We bound them." The correction was sharp. "Thirteen priestesses, one for each moon of the year. We carved limits into their very essence. They could hold territory, never expand it. Could only transform those whose spirits were willing."

I thought of Ysu in his grove—ancient, patient, and unable to leave. Of the wolf-woman and her talk of boundaries. Of how I had walked into the forest of my own accord.

"But magic has its own will," my mother continued. "The bindings we created...they changed us too. Every priestess who participated carried the mark in her blood. Our daughters would be drawn to the spirits. Would hunger for something beyond human life. Would owe a debt to the forest that helped us open the door."

The spirit before me solidified, my mother's face the one I remembered so well. "I felt it too, but then everything changed. They enslaved me, stole me from my grove, and stripped me of all that was sacred. I had no power left." Her hand lifted to cup my cheek. "But then I had you. My light in the darkness. And for a few years, I was happy. I would have lived it all again just to hold you in my arms once more." She reached for me then, but all I felt was the cold kiss of mist.

"I used what little power I had left to convince your father to adopt you. I wanted to hide you from the curse that lingered in my blood. I wanted to save you from the monsters of my past, not deliver you to new ones. I failed on both counts. I am sorry, my daughter."

"You didn't want me to become a Roman's wife?"

"I wanted to keep you. I was selfish. I wanted you to be human, as I had become. But curses cannot end in shadows. They can only end in blood."

Light glittered on her cheeks, a ghost's remorse. "Instead, my own hubris led you down a path straight to a human monster."

"His cruelty drove me straight to Ysu."

"The curse's irony. Or perhaps its intention all along." She began to fade at the edges, and I lurched toward her. My hand passed through her, and her smile held the sadness all mothers knew.

"What am I becoming?"

"What you were always meant to be. The serpent that devours its own tail, the cycle that completes itself." Her form flickered. "But know this—when you consume the one who broke you, you won't just gain power. You'll gain memory. Every woman who came before, every bargain made, every terrible price paid. The full weight of our bloodline's choices."

"And if I refuse?"

Her eyes crinkled at the corners. "You live forever incomplete, hungry for something you'll never name. We cannot escape what we are, my love. We can only choose how we embrace it."

I woke gasping on the forest floor, scales covering most of my skin, iridescent in the moonlight.

Around me, the forest waited. I felt its attention like a weight on my skin, watching to see whether plans laid over centuries would finally bear fruit.

My fingers dug into the soft earth, nails filling with dark soil. The forest thought to use me as another weapon in its centuries-old war against Rome. But as I knelt there, feeling the ground pulse beneath my palms, I recognized the truth—I would use it right back.

Every scar Tiberius carved into my flesh, every night his men held me down while he watched, every moment he tried to convince me I was nothing—all crystallized into a rage so pure it made my serpent nature seem tame by comparison. They had tried to break me. Instead, they had forged something infinitely more dangerous.

What the forest intended as its scheme would become *my* weapon. Its power would be the instrument of *my* vengeance.

I would take that very power and bend it to the revenge that had always burned brightest in my heart. Let the old magic flow through me—I would channel every drop toward the reckoning my former husband deserved.

I rose—movement halfway between standing and uncoiling—and breathed deep. The air tasted of blood, of change long foretold. Somewhere to the south, in the villa that had been my hell, waited the final piece of my becoming.

CHAPTER 21

THE SERPENT

The villa reeked of decay and madness.

I moved through corridors that had once been my prison, noting how quickly Roman order had crumbled without slaves to maintain it. Silk webs draped the corners like funeral shrouds. Dark stains marked where bodies had decayed. The halls echoed, no longer filled with anything but death.

I found Tiberius where Ysu and I had left him. Two weeks of captivity had carved away his imperial bearing. His toga hung in filthy tatters. His gray hair was matted with sweat and worse. When he heard my approach, his eyes rolled wildly before finally focusing on my transformed figure.

"Flavia?" The name came out cracked, uncertain. A name I had nearly forgotten. "Is that...gods, what have you become?"

I circled him slowly, taking in his degradation. His proud Roman features were sunken with hunger. The silk—or perhaps some older magic—had preserved him like a living mummy, keeping him alive but weak. Part of me, some remnant of the broken girl I'd once been, almost pitied him.

"Water," he croaked. "Please. Just water."

I found a pitcher still half full and held it to his lips. He drank greedily, desperately, and for a moment I saw him as merely human. Old. Frightened. Pathetic.

Then he spoke again.

"There's still time," he gasped between swallows. "Cut me free. I have gold hidden. Connections in Rome. I can help you find healers—priests who can reverse this corruption."

"Corruption?" I set the pitcher aside.

"This...curse. This demonic possession." His voice grew stronger, falling into familiar patterns of authority. "You're still Flavia beneath the scales. Still my wife I tried to civilize. We can fix this."

"Civilize." The word tasted like ash. "Is that what you called it?"

"I gave you purpose! Structure! Without me, you'd have died in some pagan hovel, bearing savage children for savage men." Spite crept into his tone, the Tiberius I knew emerging beneath the fear. "I elevated you. Made you part of the Empire to pay off my debt to your father. And this is how you repay—"

"You tortured me." My voice reverberated in my chest, and he flinched. "Systematically. Creatively. For years."

"Disciplined," he corrected, reaching for the old justifications. "Your father begged me to keep you from becoming... this. Every lesson, every correction, was to save you from the monster in your blood." His eyes raked over my scaled form with disgust. "Clearly, I was too gentle."

Too gentle. After everything—the burns, the cuts, the violations—he thought he'd been too gentle.

The last of my human pity evaporated.

"You know what my mother didn't tell my father?" I moved closer, feeling the first stirrings of the shift. "The monster was always there. You didn't prevent it. You fed it. You gave it rage to grow on. Without you, I might have stayed human."

"Barbarian whore," he spat, fear making him vicious. "I should have killed you the first time you bled on my floors. I should have—"

His words cut off as my transformation accelerated. My spine elongated with sounds like breaking branches. Scales rippled across every inch of skin. My legs fused and stretched into a serpentine tail that coiled around the room. But it was my head that changed most dramatically—jaw unhinging, throat expanding into a vast tunnel lined with backward-curving teeth.

I became what the forest had been shaping me to be. Not human. Not snake. Something between and beyond both.

Tiberius screamed then, high and thin. "Monster! Demon! When Rome hears of this—when the legions come—"

I lowered my transformed head until we were eye to eye. When I spoke, my voice was not just my own. It carried generations of women held down by weak men who feared them. It carried a forest older than man, a mind that knew more of this world than humans ever would. It carried a god who would swallow everything that stood in its way.

"Let them come."

"They will!" Even facing death, his Roman arrogance clung like mold. "Soldiers, priests, and more iron and fire than your barbarian magic can withstand. We are endless. We are order. We are—"

I wouldn't bear it a moment longer.

"Silence."

His jaw snapped shut as our gazes locked, his body going rigid beneath my command.

"You are nothing," I said. "A speck in the timeline of humanity. Your legacy is gone, and soon you will be too. But I —the barbarian girl you tried to control, I am every woman your empire ground beneath its heel, given form and fang. We do not forget. We do not forgive. We become."

He fought my control, but I was stronger. I had always been stronger. My body had finally caught up to my soul.

I wrapped my tail around his torso and squeezed until his eyes bulged. "Time for you to be prey, my dear husband."

I struck faster than lightning. My expanded jaw closed around his head and shoulders in one motion. He tried to speak as I swallowed, his muffled words vibrating through me. I felt his struggles, weak after weeks of captivity. Felt his disbelief that this was truly happening. Felt the moment he understood there would be no last-minute rescue, no divine intervention.

The silk wrapping made him easier to consume, a smooth parcel sliding down my throat. My body rippled with slow, powerful contractions, drawing him deeper. His legs kicked frantically for a heartbeat, then stilled as my venom began its work.

I took one last swallow and devoured him. Then he was gone, dissolved into the acidic darkness of my stomach. I felt his life force spreading through me, his truth dissolving into me. As I consumed him, I understood him.

He had been cruel, with crueler appetites. But his greater sin to his superiors had been his incompetence. Rather than deal with him, they'd kicked him out of Rome and given him a post at the end of the world. Out of sight, out of mind. His inferiority had festered, and it had fed his cruelty.

He was everything I had once believed myself to be—weak, pathetic, worthless. A coward who needed to hurt those who couldn't fight back to feel strong.

But I had always been stronger, and now he was nothing at all.

Beyond consuming him, I felt completion. The circle my mother's blood had started was finally closed.

Power flooded through me. Not just physical strength, but understanding. I saw my grandmother's memories, my great-grandmother's, all the way back to that first binding. I understood fully what we were, and what the forest had always intended.

My enormous tail whipped through the space, crashing into stone walls until they collapsed. This human structure was nothing, and I returned it to nothing. I slid out of the villa, bringing down everything behind me. The stone fortress crumbled around me, stones remembering they were earth, mortar returning to dust. All that remained was the mosaic on the foyer floor. Medusa's azure eyes glinted up at me, and I swore she grinned.

I raced back toward the forest, toward my true home, when I felt Tiberius' final thoughts.

The road...soldiers...they will destroy you all.

Through the chaos around me, I heard it—the steady tromp of Roman boots on stone. Many boots. An entire legion at least, marching up the road.

Tiberius had been right about one thing. Rome would not accept the loss of a villa, the death of a citizen, the whispers of monsters in the wood. They would come with iron and fire. They would try to burn out the infection they believed we represented.

I contracted back into my mostly human form, though my skin kept its scales and my eyes their serpentine cast. I took one last look at the villa. It was almost completely gone. Let it crumble. Let the forest reclaim it stone by stone.

I ran through the woods, but still felt the vibration of the legion moving across the land. I scaled a tree in three breaths, breaking through the canopy to locate them. On the road below, a column of red and bronze marched in perfect formation. At their head rode priests in white, carrying a staff crowned with the iron eagle of Rome.

As Cysgod had said, the war would claim us all, no matter our allegiance. And it was no longer coming.

It was here.

I had to warn the others.

CHAPTER 22

THE SERPENT

I found them at the old boundary where Roman stone had once cut through ancient wood. But the road was gone—or rather, transformed. Massive roots erupted through the paving stones, and trees grew in impossible tangles. The forest had reclaimed its stolen ground overnight.

"Sister!" Adda flowed from the shadows, her serpent form magnificent. Her tail was massive, covered in black-and-white striped scales that ran up her abdomen, only partially disappearing as they transitioned to bare human breasts. "You did it. I can smell it on you."

Cysgod emerged next, her pack surrounding us. "The Romans march into our trap. They expect a road. They'll find only teeth."

All around us, the transformed gathered. The bark-skinned man had sprouted branches from the top of his head, his face barely visible behind a curtain of leaves. The fox twins perched in the branches, their amber eyes gleaming with anticipation. Others I hadn't seen before—a woman whose face was dotted with raven's feathers, a man with antlers spreading from his skull like a crown.

"Where is the spider?" Adda asked, noting my solitary arrival.

"He will not come." The words hurt as they fell from my mouth.

Adda's expression softened slightly. "Then we fight without him. The forest will—"

Horns cut through the morning air. Roman horns, calling formations, signaling the advance. Through the trees, we could see them—three hundred soldiers in perfect rows, their shields locked together, their priests chanting words that made the air burn.

"Spread out," Cysgod commanded. "Use the forest. Be the shadows between leaves and the roots that trip. This is our domain."

The battle began with no fanfare, only a whisper.

A soldier stepped off what he thought was road and sank to his waist in earth that hadn't been soft moments before. Branches swung down with crushing force where no wind blew. Roots erupted to tangle feet and pierce armor gaps. The forest itself had become a weapon.

I moved through the chaos, still learning my new form. My body flowed between human and serpent, sometimes running on legs, sometimes sliding on scales. When soldiers broke formation, I was there—fangs finding arteries, venom turning their blood to fire. But I was clumsy compared to the others, still learning my gift.

That's when I saw him—the high priest, standing untouched in a circle of blessed salt. His staff glowed with light that burned away reaching vines and sent the transformed reeling. They called it holy light, but what is light without darkness? Around him, lesser priests maintained a protective chant that held the forest at bay.

Our eyes met across the battlefield. He was young for a high priest, perhaps forty, with the rough hands of one who had seen many battles. When he grinned, it held the same certainty Tiberius had worn—the absolute faith that Rome would endure.

"Demon," he called, his voice carrying despite the screams and clash of metal. "Face me."

I should have stayed with the others, used the forest's advantage. But pride—new and lethal as my fangs—drove me forward. I slithered through the melee, dodging sword strikes and pilum throws, until I stood just outside his circle.

"I am a demon created by your own hubris. Something your empire woke when it tried to tame the wild."

"All savagery falls before civilization." He raised his staff, and the eagle atop it blazed with light that made my scales burn. "Your kind is a disease. We are the cure."

I struck, but he was ready. The staff swung to meet me, its blessed metal searing through my scales. Pain, burning hot, flared across my arm. I reeled back, my form stuttering between shapes as my heart raced, my chest tight.

He advanced.

"Did you think you were powerful?" He struck again, driving me to my knees. "I have killed dozens of your kind. Burned their sacred groves and salted the ritual grounds. You are nothing but another beast to be put down."

He struck me again, and I fell to the ground. My skin burned where the iron had touched me, and it was all too familiar—the scent of burning flesh, the deep throbbing. It was pain I should have been immune to, but instead it froze me, years of memories holding me down better than any chain.

He raised the staff for a killing blow, and I saw my death in its divine light. The forest screamed around us but could not breach his protections. This was how it ended—gasping in the dirt while Rome's faith crushed the old ways once again.

The staff never fell.

A massive form descended from the trees above, eight spider limbs thrown between me and the deadly assault. He took the blow meant for me, the blessed iron sinking deep into his spider thorax. Light and darkness warred where metal met chitin, and his scream shook the very earth beneath us.

But he didn't fall. Instead, his additional arms closed around the priest like a cage. The blessed circle shattered as he skewered priest after priest on his claws. As the protective chants were silenced, the forest rushed in with all its hunger.

Ysu's mouth opened to that terrible width, and his mandibles grasped the priest's head, yanking it free of his body. He stuffed the skull into his mouth, and it crunched between his rows of teeth. Red human blood mixed with the green ichor that flowed out of Ysu, coating the forest floor.

The battle turned in an instant—Romans fleeing as their holy protection crumbled, the forest pursuing with root and fang.

But I only had eyes for Ysu as he collapsed, the ground shaking with his weight. I ran to his side, cradling his head in my arms.

"Why did you do that?" I screamed at him. "Why did you come?"

"Stupid...little serpent." His voice was weak but fond. "Of course I came. You think...anything in this world would stop me...when I felt you in danger?"

Tears I didn't know I could still cry streaked down my scaled cheeks. "I ran. I denied you. I—"

"Doesn't matter." One of his human hands found my face, claws gentle against my scales. "Even if you never chose me...I would always choose you. I would always protect you. That's what it means...to truly claim someone. To love someone. I had forgotten that."

His chest shook as he took deep breaths. "I'm sorry, my neidr. You were right. I was afraid. Afraid that the most beautiful creature who has ever come into my life would leave me to my hunger. I knew it would devour me if I didn't have you by my side. But I hurt you in a way you did not wish to be hurt, and for that I should not be forgiven."

Around us, Roman survivors fled down paths that twisted back on themselves, their screams filling the air, but I barely noticed, focused only on the ancient creature dying in my arms.

"Don't," I begged. "You arrogant arachnid. Don't talk like...like you're leaving me."

"The forest has you now." Each breath rasped through his chest, weaker than the last. "And you...you have yourself. That's all I ever wanted...for you to know your own strength."

"Ysu—"

"Though if you wanted...to choose me now..." His mandibles clicked weakly in what might have been humor. "I wouldn't...object."

I pressed my forehead to his. "I choose you. Not from gratitude or broken need. I choose you as you chose me—to keep."

"Pretty words...for a pretty serpent." But his eyes brightened slightly, then dimmed again. One by one, his eight eyes began to close, the light fading from each like stars winking out at dawn.

"No." The word tore from me with a force that shook the trees. "You don't get to die now." I refused. I *refused*. I cried out in anguish, holding him so tight a normal man would have been crushed. He was mine. I refused to let him go.

The memories of my ancestors returned to me. That fateful night when they had given hunger earthly form through an arrogant warlord. The spirit consumed him as the priestess chanted, "Take this vessel, be bound to mortal form, but know this—as we give, so must you. Blood for blood, venom for venom."

Ysu's breathing grew shallow, the wound from the blessed iron spreading corruption through his ancient form. Green ichor pooled beneath us, soaking into earth.

"Some things...even monsters...cannot survive," he whispered.

"You're wrong." I shifted him in my arms, leaning over him. "You claimed me with venom. Made me yours."

"Yes..." His voice was fading.

"But I never claimed you." I leaned closer, feeling my fangs extend, venom sacs swelling. "You marked me...saved me. Now it's my turn."

His eyes widened slightly as understanding dawned.

I pressed my hand to his chest, feeling his ancient heart stuttering. "You are mine, Ysu. My guardian, my chosen. And I will not let you die."

He was weak, but he nodded. My fangs found the soft flesh where his human neck met spider armor, sinking deep.

He convulsed, all eight legs thrashing as my venom met his. Where the blessed iron had poisoned, my gift purified. Where the priest's faith had wounded, my claim mended. I felt the connection between us shift and complete—no longer one-sided possession but mutual claiming.

The creatures of the forest held their breath as I poured everything into him—my rage, my venom, my love. Yes, love. I could name it now, this feeling that transcended hunger or need. The venom carried it all, rewriting his wounds into wholeness.

When I finally pulled back, dizzy from the effort, his eyes were open again. All eight of them, brighter than before, with flecks of gold that matched mine.

"You bit me," he said, a wicked smile on his face.

"I claimed you." I helped him up, marveling at how the terrible wound had closed, leaving only a scar that mimicked the pattern of my scales. "The spider and the serpent, bound by venom but together by choice."

He touched the mark my fangs had left, and I saw something I'd never seen in his ancient features—surprise. "I can feel it. Your venom, not changing me, but..."

"Completing you. As yours completed me. Helped me become my true self." I smiled, tasting his ichor on my fangs.

Around us, the forest bristled with satisfaction, quite pleased with itself.

Ysu pulled me against him. "My fierce serpent."

I traced the new mark on his chest, watching it shimmer with the shadow of iridescent scales.

The forest erupted in celebration—trees swaying without wind, flowers blooming out of season, the very air singing with approval. The Romans were forgotten, fled into a land that would never again be theirs. What mattered was the power we had awakened not only in the forest, but between us. The curse of my ancestors remained, but it had been reborn into something new. Something with fangs that could protect this world as they had always intended.

"So"—Ysu's mandibles clicked with a sound I had not heard before, joy—"what shall we do with forever, my neidr?"

I grinned, showing fangs. "Hunt. Protect what's ours. Together."

"Together," he agreed. "But you have been gone from my web for quite some time. I have many ways in which I must ensure you do not leave my side again." He slung me over his shoulder, and I did not protest.

The war would continue. Rome would send more soldiers, more priests. But we would be ready—not as guardian and victim, not as predator and prey, but as equals bound by choice and strengthened by ancient purpose.

The serpent had swallowed its tail. The spider had woven his web.

And in the heart of the ancient forest, two monsters transformed what was once a curse into a new beginning.

EPILOGUE

THE SPIDER - 50 YEARS LATER

My web stretched between trees that had not existed a year before, the silver strands catching the light of the full moon. My serpent hung suspended at the center, her silver scales gleaming with an iridescent sheen. Her hair caught the light in the same way, and her golden eyes followed my every move.

"Comfortable?" I inquired, moving behind her, where her gaze could not follow.

"A bit too comfortable, perhaps," she teased, snapping a few of the bonds. It was easy for her now, a reminder of the gift she gave me when she allowed me to bind her.

"Always a glutton for punishment, my hungry serpent." I traced my claws along her sinuous tail and buried my nose in the soft strands of her hair. I brushed a finger over the scar on her chest—my mark—a mirror of the web that held her. No longer a sign of possession, but of a promise between two creatures who had chosen eternity together.

"I'm always curious to see what you come up with." She turned her head, capturing my lips with hers, our tongues entangling until my whole body burned with need. But we had all the time in the world; there was no need to rush.

"Do you know what the wolf told me yesterday?" I asked.

My serpent frowned as I pulled away from her. Always so impatient. "Which wolf? The territory is crawling with them now." She shifted in the bonds, not to escape but to feel the silk slide against her scales. "Ever since you let them den in the northern groves—"

"Cysgod said the Romans have a new name for this place." She was moving too much. I tied more silk around her, slowly, watching her pupils widen with need. "Silva Devoratrix. The Devouring Forest."

"Fitting," she gasped as I tightened a knot over a particularly sensitive spot we had discovered on her tail. "How many legions have fed the roots now? Four? Five?"

"Six. Though the last hardly counted. They fled before crossing the boundary stones." I leaned closer, my mandibles clicking near her ear. "The stories the survivors spread have done more than any battle. Entire regions avoid the deep woods now."

"Our reputation precedes us," she said, arching into my touch. "The spider and the serpent. Guardians of the expanding wild."

"Is that what we are? Guardians?" I chuckled, my thoughts darkening as she writhed in my grip. "I thought we were monsters."

"To humans, is there a difference?" She smiled wide, her fangs dripping with sweet venom. I leaned in and licked it, my tongue catching on the tip of her fang until the taste of iron filled both our mouths. She moaned so sweetly I knew I wouldn't be able to tease her much longer. Fifty years hadn't diminished the hunger between us—if anything, our mutual claiming had deepened it, made it something richer, more complex.

"Ysu…" she growled, and more of my web snapped as she writhed with impatience.

"Always so hungry."

"You made me this way."

"Oh no, my serpent—we both know you were always insatiable." I ran my hands down the smooth scales at her waist, where they still merged with soft human skin. Lower and lower I ventured until I found the place where they parted, revealing her deep heat to me.

I pressed aside the scales covering her slit and plunged my clawed fingers into the velvety confines of her cunt. She threw her head back against my shoulder, panting.

"Not enough, Ysu…"

"Insatiable."

I used my legs to adjust the web, spinning her until she whipped around, suspended upside down. Her face was now level with my fully emerged cocks. She immediately wrapped her long, forked tongue around one, and I watched her try to free an arm from her bindings to toy with the other.

Instead, two of my limbs bound her tighter. She groaned in frustration, and the sound only sent more precum dripping down her cheeks and into her hot mouth.

I had long ago stopped needing to be gentle with her, especially not when she was like this. I thrust in until I felt the tight ring at the back of her throat, and her tongue followed the twisted grooves as I pulled back again.

My claws found the back of her head, holding her still as I fucked deeper into her throat, opening her. I felt her jaw unlatch, and when I pushed back in, she took both of my cocks into her mouth.

"You're perfect," I groaned against the scales of her hip before my own long tongue pushed its way inside her. Her taste satisfied my hunger as nothing else ever had, and as I drew back, circling the soft bud hidden beneath her scales, she hummed around me.

It wasn't long before my knots began to swell, and as divine as her mouth felt, I knew we both needed more.

I manipulated my web again until she was upright, her eyes dazed with the rush of blood and lust. Her lips were swollen and dotted with tiny beads of blood, and I licked them off, tasting her and me and the sweet venom that sang between us.

"My arrogant spider, my light in the darkness," she murmured, giving me a lazy smile, "kiss me and tell me you love me."

I kissed her deep, every single one of my limbs holding her close, except the hand that held my cocks together as I pushed into the tight entrance of her slit.

She moaned into my mouth as I seated fully inside her. "I love you, my serpent." I pulled out and slammed back in. "You brought me back to life when there was nothing but the void, and you showed me what true strength was."

"Ysu..." Her eyes rolled back, and I felt her tightening around me even as I began to swell. "Tell me you're mine."

Her whole body shook, my bindings snapping one by one. I wrapped her in my arms as she came undone, feeling the pleasure crash through her. I thrust into that perfect, velvety heat one last time as I followed her over the edge. My knots caught inside her, and that last bit of pressure had wave after wave of cum pouring into her. "I'm yours, my serpent. And I would tear apart the very web of reality to hold you in my arms."

Now I was the one trembling, and as I filled her, she sank her fangs into my shoulder, completing the cycle as she pumped her venom into me. It amplified the pleasure until I was completely lost in bliss, the light of the moon splitting into prismatic colors as every part of me was filled with her. I wanted nothing else.

When we had both come down from the high of lust and venom, she freed herself from the last of her bindings and curled against my chest, her tail wrapping around my waist. "And I am yours, Ysu. This forest may have called me, but you made me want to stay. I was taught to fear monsters, but you taught me to fear nothing at all. I love you Ysu, from now until the last star falls from the sky."

———

A Roman Children's Folk Song (c. 323 AD)

When moonlit scales gleam in the night,
beware the Serpent's hungry bite.

She calls with eyes of molten gold,
to lure the young, the lost, the bold.

Beside her waits her Spider King;
Together, death is what they bring.

So keep to paths both straight and true,
lest ancient hunger Devour you.

Thank You!

Thank you so much for reading this book! If you loved it, please consider leaving a review on Amazon or any other review platform. Reviews are crucial to small indie authors like myself. Any time you take is greatly appreciated.

If you want to know what's coming next, consider signing up for my newsletter or following me on Instagram.

Love the book and what your own gorgeous Deluxe edition (and support me directly)? Take a look on my website.

www.avathorne.com

About the Author

Ava Thorne is a lover of fantastical stories of all genres, but especially when they involve complex (and often hot) characters falling in love.

She lives in the Southwestern United States with her husband and two children. She loves the desert and drinking matcha lattes while dreaming up her next world.

She can always be found at www.avathorne.com

Other Works by the Author:

The Embers of Magic Duology
Born of Mist and Dragonfire
Rising from Flames and Starlight

The Neo Stellaris Series
Neon Flux
Electric High - Coming soon

Pythonissam Filia Series
Devoured
Possessed - Coming soon

ACKNOWLEDGMENTS

As always, huge shout out to my partner for always being the most supportive husband a girl can ask for, even when I just want to write a book about the hot spider demon in the woods.

Thank you to my beta readers Jasi and Caroline. You really helped me clean this up and solidify Flavia's journey.

To my street team and ARC readers, thank you so much for giving this book the hype it deserved.

And always, last but not least, to Daniel Deluxe for creating the best hyper focus music known to man.

www.ingramcontent.com/pod-product-compliance
Lightning Source LLC
Chambersburg PA
CBHW020052310726
48970CB00007B/2529